Robert Campbell

JOURNEY to HARE ISLAND

A Tale of the Bras D'Or

ROBERT L. CAMPBELL

◆ FriesenPress

Suite 300 - 990 Fort St
Victoria, BC, Canada, V8V 3K2
www.friesenpress.com

Copyright © 2015 by Robert L. Campbell
First Edition — 2015

Cover Photo by the author.
Maps by Jessica Campbell.

All rights reserved.

No part of this publication may be reproduced in any form, or by any means, electronic or mechanical, including photocopying, recording, or any information browsing, storage, or retrieval system, without permission in writing from FriesenPress.

ISBN
978-1-4602-7339-5 (Hardcover)
978-1-4602-7340-1 (Paperback)
978-1-4602-7341-8 (eBook)

1. Fiction

Distributed to the trade by The Ingram Book Company

Dedication

To Ian, David, Bob, and Lynn, who heard a few stories;
to Jessica and Ethan, the next generation;
and, of course, to Fran.

Acknowledgements

The myth of the "hero's journey" is outlined in the works of Joseph Campbell. The description of how the "moon hare" originated is Rowan's version of a tale from Buddhist tradition.

I would like to thank the people at Friesen Press for their guidance as this book was being readied for publication, especially the efficient and courteous Code Workun.

PREFACE

The Bras D'Or Lakes are large, interconnected bodies of salt water in the centre of Cape Breton Island. They are joined to the Atlantic by two natural channels in the east and by a canal in the southwest.

The Bras D'Or watershed, renowned for its physical beauty, has been home to the Mi'kmaq people since prehistoric times, and their spiritual connection to the Lakes and surrounding lands is very strong. In the eighteenth century, French settlers came to the St Peter's area, where some managed to stay despite deportations and the fall of Louisbourg. Then in the nineteenth century, large numbers of Highland Scots settled along the Lakes, and although farming the rugged landscape provided only a modest living, they came to love their new home.

Economic imperatives after the Second World War made farming on the Bras D'Or watershed less attractive, and many people were forced to leave for other parts of North America. Unworked farms reverted to a wilder state, with vegetation in some sections characterized by white spruce and alder, and in others by hardwoods. Through all of this, one resident of the watershed, the snowshoe hare (*Lepus americanus*), ignored economics and continued to flourish.

The snowshoe hare is more inclined than the common English hare to live in bush-covered rather than open areas, and it has a more compact body shape, so English speakers in Canada erroneously labelled it a "rabbit." But it is a true hare: Its young (*leverets*) are born with fur and with eyes open, ready to face the world much quicker than their rabbit cousins.

Like most hares, snowshoe hares are most active in early morning and late evening, but they can often be seen in daylight hours, especially during breeding periods. When not out feeding, they retreat to the bushes, where they use habitual resting places called *forms,* often slight depressions in the ground. Trails in the vicinity of their forms are termed *runs.*

Stories involving hares appear in mythologies around the world, and I have taken the liberty of placing our snowshoe hare within this broad context.

The hares from this story are here each day outside my country home; I can see them from my front window.

Robert L. Campbell
Johnstown, Nova Scotia

JOURNEY
to HARE ISLAND

A Tale of the Bras D'Or

Chapter 1
AUTUMN VISIT

The Otter walked up to this chief and made inquiries. "Did you see a Hare running in this direction, carrying a string of eels? I tracked him to this village." "Hare! Hare!" said the chief, with a ... puzzled look: "What kind of thing is that?"
—Silas Rand, Legends Of The Micmacs

The old man leaned back in his chair, put his feet up on the railing of the deck, and sniffed the salt air: It smelled of spent leaves and dying seaweed. At the mouth of the cove to the west, terns patrolled the calm waters, their piercing cries echoing out over a broad expanse of the Bras D'Or.

Way off to his left and on the edge of the lake was the lighthouse near the opening to St Peter's Inlet, and to the north of that, the mouth of West Bay. East from there along the horizon, past Marble Mountain and the old Mi'kmaq lands at Malagawatch, were distant blue-tinted hills that showed where Whycocomagh and Baddeck fronted other sections of the lake.

The screen door banged behind him. "What's up, Grampy?" asked his grandson, as he threw himself into a deck chair next to his grandfather.

"Not much, Evan; I'm just looking at the lake. Next summer we'll do some mucking around in the boat. You kids ready for Halloween?"

"Sure; I'm gonna be a ghost. Meme promised you'd drive us around; she doesn't think we should walk on the highway."

"No problem; I know just where we'll go."

Evan's face brightened and he pointed as he said, "Look, Grampy, there's a rabbit down by the alders." There it was: brownish fur and long ears, bending its head to pluck grass and then sitting up to chew and watch for danger.

"Not many around," said Grampy.

"How come?"

The old man shrugged his shoulders and pulled down his cap to block out the setting sun. "Predators, disease, not enough food—their numbers crash every ten years or so. Even the experts aren't sure why."

"You mean they just die?"

"Quite a few do. In fact, I know a story about that, if you and Tessie could chuck your gadgets long enough to listen."

"Great, a story. Is it true or made up?"

Grampy laughed. "I've been around rabbits so long I almost know what they're thinking. One day about two years ago, I was in the garden pulling the last of the onions. A rabbit came up real close. He had a scar on his cheek where something had swatted him; he was a nice-looking rabbit with fur lighter brown than most."

"Wasn't he scared?"

"Of me? No. I don't bother them. They're pests, but I don't have the heart to shoot them; I fence with chicken wire. I run through a lot of wire, but the rabbits and my garden are still here."

Journey *to* Hare Island

He pointed to a small garden off to the right. "See the fence all around?"

"Doesn't Bodie chase them away?" asked Evan, nodding toward the Border Terrier stretched out on the deck. The dog raised its tousled grey head at the sound of its name, then sank back with a sigh.

"She just chases squirrels—not that she catches any. She'll chase rabbits if they're right out front here, but she won't go into the alders."

Grampy leaned back and put his hands behind his head. "Anyway, that day in the garden the rabbit came right up to the fence. He looked me in the eye like he was trying to tell me something. Struck me so odd, I dreamed about him that night and woke up with this story in my head. Put there by the rabbit, maybe." He looked over at Evan.

Evan laughed. "Come on, Grampy, rabbits don't tell stories. Wait a minute, *rabbits?* What did you say yesterday?"

"I was afraid you'd remember that. Okay, so they're snow-shoe hares, not rabbits."

"I remember exactly what you said: Rabbits are born helpless, like kittens, but hares are born with their eyes open, and they can move around right away."

"I know what I said, but we call them *rabbits* around here."

"Grampy, if you were a hare and not a rabbit, what would you want to be called?"

The old man chuckled. "Okay, I give up; this story is for you and Tessie, so they'll be hares. I guess Tessie would approve."

"Approve of what?" Tessie came out on the deck. She was two years younger than Evan but with the same roguish smile, a gift from her Celtic ancestors.

"Grampy'll tell us a story about snowshoe hares," said Evan. "Does that sound okay?"

"Sure," said Tessie, "but Grampy, is this story sad? I don't want a really sad story."

"Now that's a good question, Tessie. They do have enemies, and there aren't many around some years, as I was telling Evan. I'd say it's mostly happy, but you'll have to decide that for yourselves. Now you two go in; get ready for bed, and I'll be there in a minute to start the story. It's long, but you guys will be here four more days, so we'll have time to finish it."

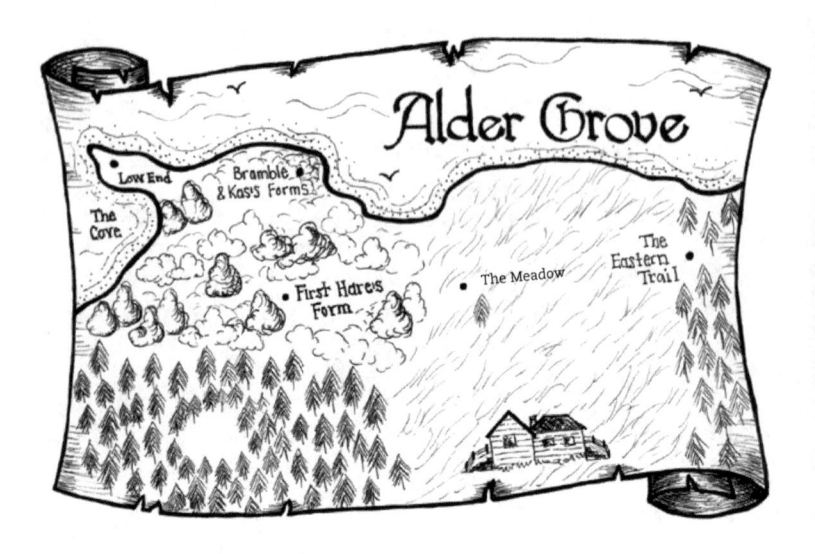

Chapter 2
THE MEADOW

My Poem for Alder Grove:
Lake wind and rain.
Thunder on summer evenings.
Meadow grass.
Moonlight shining through alder leaves.
Sparrows.
Waves.
And my friend Bram.
—Kas

First light found the snowshoe hares of Alder Grove spread out over the lake meadow, quiet silhouettes alone or in groups of two or three. Fall rain had kept the grass a tempting green, and the hares were busy eating before daylight forced them back to the bushes.

Two youngsters from late-summer litters chased each other on the western edge of the meadow, having fun and strengthening their leg muscles in the process. The adult hares fed, but their ears moved forward and back, sometimes independent of each other, always listening; any sound hinting of danger would clear the meadow. They liked mornings or evenings to be windless so they could hear approaching predators. When wind came whistling in from the lake, or when it rained heavily, the hares stayed in the bushes that made up Alder Grove. This morning all they could hear was the rhythmic sound of tiny waves meeting the shore of the lake and the mewing of herring gulls patrolling the shoreline.

As Bramble left the alders, he saw his friend Kas browsing near the edge of the bank that fronted the lake. Every so often Kas raised his head, looked around, and wrinkled his nose to test the air, but mostly he ate.

Two hares approached Kas. They had their backs turned to Bramble, but he was close enough to hear what they said: "Hey you, fat one, what are you doing on our favourite spot?" They moved in close to Kas, one on each side, and began to shoulder him.

Neither of the two hares noticed Bramble approaching from behind. He moved around the trio until they could all see him and sat on his haunches. "Well, if it isn't Sprucie and Tosh. What are you up to, fellows?"

It was one thing to bully Kas, but Bramble was another matter. They stopped what they were doing and began to move away. The one called Sprucie tried to maintain a brave front, though. "What business is it of yours, Swampie? We were just playing around."

Bramble's ears went back, but his voice stayed calm. "Go play somewhere else and leave Kas alone; you don't own this patch."

They went off, snickering, and Bramble turned to Kas. "Don't mind those two, but I thought you were going to wait for me before coming out."

Kas was hunched down, his long ears lying flat on his brown shoulders. "You were asleep, and I was hungry," he mumbled.

"Kas, when are you not hungry?"

"Doesn't matter what time I come out; Rat Face finds a way to embarrass me anyway. He hates both of us, but he's scared of you."

Bramble started to laugh. "*Rat Face,* where'd you get that name?"

A smile lit up Kas's face. "Just thought it up; does it fit?"

"Perfectly," Bramble said. "I should've swatted him when he called me Swampie." Bramble rubbed a scar on his cheek, remembering when an owl had killed his mother and sent him scrambling into the swamp. "Anyway, let's forget Sprucie. You're too bright to pay attention to a dummy like him."

"Watch your back is all I'm saying," said Kas.

The two settled down to eat, ignoring a small band of crows that landed near them on the meadow. Finally, their bellies full, they sat together looking out at the lake. Two cormorants came arrowing in and landed in the cove. One, then the other, dove in search of fish, leaving widening ripples on the water's surface. The cormorants would feed all day, but the growing light would soon drive Bramble and Kas to their forms; in fact, the younger hares had already stopped their games and moved in under the alders.

"Let's go in, Bram," said Kas. "That dumb dog will soon be out."

Bramble turned around and surveyed the meadow. Suddenly, he sat higher on his haunches and froze. "Wait a minute—who's that under the spruce?" His eyes were fixed on the single tree out on the meadow. "Is that Petal? What's she doing way out there when it's getting light?"

Other hares had noticed Bramble's stance and were looking out toward the spruce tree, and some of them, including

Flair, came running over. "Who's that out there, Bramble?" she asked.

"Petal. She must be asleep."

Flair was one of Petal's oldest friends. "Someone has to go see what's wrong," she pleaded. Flair was too old to go herself, and no one else offered. When Bramble looked around, most of the hares were looking at him. He sighed but finally moved toward the spruce tree. "Okay, I'll wake her up."

Kas called after him, "Hurry, Bram! Something will see you."

At the edge of the field, some hares ran nervously into the alders and out again. Others sat in one place, ready to bolt at any sign of danger. Bramble reached the spruce tree. "Petal, are you asleep? You have to move." She sat there with a dazed look on her greyish brown face. Did she hear him? Bramble saw movement at a front window of the house, hesitated a moment, and then raced back toward the alders.

Anxious comments came from the few hares left in the field: "What's wrong with her, Bramble?" "What can we do?"

Bramble shook his head in frustration. "She's awake, but she won't move. She'll be a goner if she stays out there." There was no more movement from the house, so Bramble went cautiously back out to the spruce tree. "This is it, Petal, you've got to come." Just then the door of the house opened, and a black and grey dog came out to the deck. It looked around, but Petal and Bramble were motionless under the spruce tree, so it didn't notice them.

Petal's nose twitched; she had scented the dog. She let out a low moan. "Bramble, I can't see very well. What'll I do?"

"It's okay," said Bramble. "I'm right here in front of you; follow me and I'll take you home." He started slowly on a direct line to the closest alders, and at last Petal began to follow.

Journey *to* Hare Island

The dog's head came up when it saw them move, and it jumped down from the deck. Petal was very slow. Bramble knew he could outrun the dog, but he couldn't bring himself to leave Petal. Then from the corner of his eye, he saw another hare dash out in front of the dog, then turn and scramble back toward the alders. It was Kas. The dog stopped, looked at the intruder, and then back at Bramble and Petal, but by then they were disappearing into the bushes. The dog stared for a brief time at the alders, then turned and went back to the house.

A breeze was drifting in from the lake, and the taller grasses swayed invitingly, but there were no hares left anywhere on the meadow.

Under the canopy of bushes, Bramble was surrounded by a group of hares. Petal had been led away to her form by Flair. A few hares had seen the narrow escape and spread the word. One was Bramble's friend Shiver. "You saved her Bramble, but weren't you scared?"

"To the tips of my ears," said Bramble, "but it was Kas who saved both of us." Kas sat there, trying hard not to grin. Off to the side, Bramble noticed Sprucie turn abruptly and make his way into a tangle of wild roses.

Later that morning, Bramble and Kas were lying quietly in their forms, close enough to the lake to hear the waves and smell the salt air. The excitement had faded, but not the concern for Petal. In the past, both had seen hares torn by predators and heard their dying screams, but neither had experienced sickness.

They tensed when they heard movement on the nearby run, but then they heard a familiar voice. "Are you fellows in there?" It was Stormy, helper to the First Hare.

Kas answered, "We're here, Stormy. Come in. Have you heard how Petal is?"

"Not good. She's very sick, and some others may be sick as well. The First Hare has called a gathering for the clearing tonight; I'm just here to give you the word. See you later." He left, and they heard him scurrying down the run.

"What do you suppose the meeting is about?" asked Kas.

Bramble shrugged. "Guess we'll have to go to find out."

Chapter 3
THE WARNING

In the spruce forest south of Alder Grove, under a full moon, hares moved silently through patterns of light and shadow. A hundred feet into the forest was a glade carpeted with grass and open to the moonlight. This was the meeting place, but it wasn't used often because hares were solitary by nature. In the glade, a rough circle of hares started to form, and the circle widened as more arrived. They were nervous in the spruce glade; they missed the canopy of alders that was usually over their heads. Tonight they were doubly nervous because word of Petal's sickness had gotten around.

As Bramble and Kas moved into the western side of the circle, Strawberry, a doe who always led the chanting, began a familiar chant:

> *Hares that form the Alder Band,*
> *In a circle now we stand.*
> *Proud companions of the night,*
> *We ask the moon to give us light*
> *So we can welcome our First Hare*
> *And in his timeless wisdom share.*

Fox and coyote, lynx and owl,
Things that fly or creep or prowl,
May your kills tonight be made
In some other, distant, forest glade.

As the chant ended, a hush came over the gathering, and into the circle came the First Hare. He was stooped, with years etched around his eyes and muzzle. He moved slowly, occasionally nodding to old friends as he went. He reached the centre and climbed the mound from which he always spoke.

The moon had now cleared the tall spruce to the south and was shining directly down on the clearing. The hares were still, a ring of golden statues bathed by the moonlight. The First Hare surveyed the gathering for a few moments and then began to speak. "Friends, I have bad news. One of our older hares, Petal, died late this evening." Bramble's shoulders sank, and he felt Kas touch one of his front paws. The First Hare continued, "Two hares who live near Petal are also sick. Aside from the suffering of these three friends, there is a more general concern, and it is my job to explain why.

"Breaker, who was First Hare when I was young, once said that he had lived through a winter of great hardship here at Alder Grove. A few hares got sick in the fall, and when winter came the sickness spread quickly. By spring, there were many empty forms. He called it *the great terror,* and said that such *terrors* have happened every few years going back to the earliest days of Alder Grove."

Here the old hare bowed his head for a moment, then continued, "Recent years have been good ones. Food has been abundant, and our numbers have grown. Sadly, we are now so many that there may not be enough food this winter, especially if the weather is bad. If this happens, our weakened condition will make us easy targets for sickness and for the creatures that prey on us. I have been dreading the arrival of such a time, but the signs are clear: Given Petal's death and the illness of the other two, I'm afraid the *terror* is on its way. I don't say this to frighten you, but to urge you to be brave and work hard to survive until spring. There must always be hares in Alder Grove. That is all I have to say."

As the First Hare made his way slowly out of the circle and was escorted back toward Alder Grove, the circle itself began to lose its form. Only one voice was raised: "But he could be wrong; perhaps none of this will happen!" No one else took up the cry; it was a fearful group that made its way home. Above the hares' heads, clouds now covered the moon, and the tops of the spruce trees shivered with a growing wind.

Bramble and Kas had reached the run near their forms when Stormy came from a side run and hailed them. "Excuse me, fellows. The First Hare would like to speak to you, Bramble."

Bramble stopped, looked at Stormy, and sat back on his haunches. "Me? He knows who I am? What does he want?"

"I have no idea, but given tonight's news, I'm sure it's important. Come with me."

They started to move off, but then Bramble stopped again. "What about Kas?"

"He only asked for you, Bramble."

Bramble looked over at Kas and shrugged. "I'll see you in a bit," he told Kas. Then he followed Stormy into the night.

Chapter 4
THE QUEST

Dry alder leaves
Rattle in the autumn wind,
Then fall.
—Kas

As Stormy and Bramble approached the centre of Alder Grove, they could hear the alder leaves shaking; even stronger winds were coming, and there would be no hares on the meadow tomorrow morning. Stormy led Bramble into a thicket of wild roses, which opened to a clearing where the youngster found himself face to face with the First Hare. Up close Bramble could clearly see the lines of age and concern on the dignified face. He bowed his head and backed away a few steps. "Excuse me, First Hare," he said.

"Don't be shy, Bramble. We haven't met, so let me look at you; they told me I'd know you by the scar on your cheek?"

Bramble touched the scar with a paw. The old hare looked over at his helper. "Thanks for bringing him, Stormy. Go get some rest; Trim will be outside in case I need anything."

Stormy bowed his head and left, and the First Hare turned again to Bramble. "You're one of the strongest and fastest of the young hares, your friends say. Judging by what you did for Petal this morning, you're brave as well."

Bramble's brow furrowed. "I didn't feel brave at the gathering."

"Well, you should be proud about this morning, Bramble; Petal died later, it's true, but she was surrounded by her friends, not alone and mauled by that dog." He lowered his voice. "Bramble, did you get close to Petal?"

"Not really," said Bramble. "I just talked to her."

"Very good; if you get close to a sick hare, you can get sick yourself. We need you well, Bramble, because I hope you'll do something for Alder Grove." The old hare nodded his head. "Yes, the *terror* is surely coming; we'll have a difficult winter." He hesitated a moment and looked up at the dying leaves swaying in the wind, then his voice brightened. "Do you know who Shadow was, Bramble?"

"Yes, he lived a long time ago. I don't know what he did, but everyone respected him. He became a First Hare, didn't he?"

"Yes, he did, but earlier he had gone on a journey for Alder Grove, and it was just before a *terror*. I'm going to ask you to go on just such a journey."

Bramble sat up abruptly. "But I don't know anything about journeys." His voice changed almost to a whisper. "All I know is Alder Grove."

"I understand, Bramble; you're very young. I wouldn't ask you if this wasn't important, and if I didn't think you were the right one to send." He looked around, as if searching for words, then continued, "Our lake stretches a long way eastward, toward the morning sun. Trails in that direction are difficult, and many creatures that prey on us live there, including man."

Bramble pushed down on his front paws to hide his trembling.

"I don't deny there'll be dangers, Bramble. You'll follow the shore a long way and travel by day because you won't know the trails. Eventually you'll see an island with a hill on its western end. Surprisingly, Bramble, the island is called *Hare Island*." The First Hare smiled and studied Bramble. "It won't be easy to get there, and some Island hares might think you carry disease; you'll have to persuade them that you don't. Their healer, or their First Hare, should understand our difficulties and give you something to take home. Finally, it's important that you stay on Hare Island for the winter and return here only in the spring. Is that clear?"

Brambles legs were weak. A journey? He didn't want to go on a journey. The sides of the clearing seemed to be closing in on him, and he swallowed to keep down his fear. He hadn't really agreed to go, but the First Hare seemed to think he had. Could a youngster turn down a request from his First Hare?

"I can't tell you much more now, Bramble." The First Hare looked with sad old eyes at the young hare. "But our future may depend on you."

He was about to continue when there was a commotion at the entrance and a young hare was pushed into the clearing. Behind him came Trim, one of the First Hare's guards. "I'm sorry to interrupt," Trim said, "but this hare was lurking outside, listening to your conversation."

The First Hare's voice turned hard. "Thank you for being so alert, Trim. Wait outside while I deal with this." He turned abruptly to the intruder. "What's the meaning of this? Who are you?"

Journey *to* Hare Island

Surprisingly, the answer came from Bramble: "I'm sorry, First Hare, but this is my friend Kas."

Kas said meekly, "I was only trying to find my friend."

The First Hare looked over at Bramble. "Did you put him up to this?"

Bramble shook his head.

The old hare looked at Kas. "What can I do with you, you foolish hare? You had no business spying on us; the other hares won't understand why I've sent Bramble on a journey, and that will only add to their worry."

Bramble wanted to counter the First Hare's anger, but before he could say anything, Kas said, "I want to go with Bramble."

Even Bramble was surprised, and the First Hare said, "Ridiculous! This journey is for one hare only."

Bramble had visions of Kas being driven out of Alder Grove or worse. He groped for a way to protect his friend: "Kas and I are always together, First Hare, and we've been friends for a long time, and he helped me save Petal this morning, and so if he really wants to go?"

Bramble and Kas both lowered their heads as the First Hare looked from one to the other. When Bramble finally glanced up, the First Hare's expression had softened. "So be it," the First Hare agreed. "Against my better judgement, your friend may go, Bramble, but only because I'm asking so much of you." He turned to Kas and said, "What you did was wrong, but if I had a friend as loyal as you two seem to be to each other, I guess I'd stick close as well."

The First Hare rose and ushered them outside. "I'll get Stormy to take you to the east side of the Grove and point you in the right direction. He'll make sure you aren't followed."

"But do we have to go right away?" Bramble asked. "Can't we say goodbye to our friends?"

"Have no contact with anyone else here, please, and avoid strange hares along the way; you could get the sickness from them. I'm afraid you'll have to leave immediately."

He led the two friends to a nearby form and talked for a few moments with Stormy before going back to his clearing. Stormy took them toward the eastern edge of the Grove. The dry leaves of the alder trees scraped and scratched together in the autumn wind, and the two youngsters looked around fearfully, imagining owls and coyotes. When they reached the meadow, Stormy pointed across the way and said, "You'll see two taller trees on the edge of the forest; go between them, and you'll find a path leading east."

Before Stormy could turn away, Bramble asked, "But why this journey, Stormy? I don't understand."

"I only know he thinks it's important. Good luck to both of you." Stormy turned and went back into the Grove, leaving Bramble and Kas gazing eastward into the darkness. Alder leaves, freed by the wind, drifted past their heads and disappeared over the meadow. Finally Bramble whispered, "Let's at least see what's on the other side; I've never been over there."

Meanwhile, back in Alder Grove, the First Hare and Stormy sat facing each other in the old hare's clearing. "Did they say anything more about the journey?" the First Hare asked.

"As you predicted, Bramble asked why they were going."

"And you answered?""

"I said I didn't know, and I felt guilty lying. Do you think those two will survive going to Hare Island and back?"

"Stormy, if the *terror* comes this winter, will any of us survive?"

Chapter 5
FIRST NIGHT

Wings of the night owl,
Silent and strong,
Float on the dark wind.
—Kas

Wind made the taller grasses sway, and the grass brushed the youngsters' sides as they crossed the meadow. When they reached the far side, they gazed up at the tops of the spruce trees. "Makes me dizzy, they're so tall," said Kas. "Give me alders any time."

"We'll probably see stranger sights than this," said Bramble, "and once we start down this trail, there's no turning back."

"It's not that I want to go so much, Bram; it's that I don't want to stay. Who knows what Sprucie would do? I know I'm a coward."

"So who saved my skin this morning with that dog?" Bramble stood and looked between the two trees. "We might as well find out what's in there, and Kas, I'm glad you're with me."

They started eastward into the forest, keeping the lake to their left, and followed the trail until they began to get weary. It had rained enough to soak their fur. Tired and wet, they looked

Journey *to* Hare Island

for shelter. They found a place to huddle under the lower branches of a spruce tree. They had just settled down when they heard, from close by, the hoot of an owl. Bramble rubbed at the scar on his cheek without thinking. Kas mumbled, "I don't think an owl could find us under here, could it?"

"We're both young and healthy; we can run if we have to."

"Run?" said Kas. "You must be thinking of another friend, a thin one." Kas waddled around, making Bramble laugh even though he could hardly see Kas in the gloom.

Rain made a hissing sound as it hit the evergreens, but only an occasional drop got through the branches over their heads. They made themselves as comfortable as possible on the thick moss. But Kas couldn't sleep, and he whispered, "Bram, I just thought of something: When I'm going to sleep at home, I have a picture of the entire Grove that runs in my head. If something came after me, a coyote or whatever, I'd know exactly where to run. I'm picturing those runs now, but what good will it do here or anywhere but the Grove?"

"You're right, Kas, it'll all be scary, but right now we have to sleep."

Then, closer this time, the owl hooted again.

Kas got up and stared into the open space just beyond their shelter. Suddenly he froze and whispered, "Do you see something out there?"

Bramble looked toward the clearing but could see only the dark outlines of trees in the background. "Relax and stop imagining things."

But Kas kept staring into the clearing, and whispered again, "Please take another look."

Bramble grumbled, but he got up and looked harder into the gloom. He tensed; Kas was right. A dark something was standing not far from their tree, and even as he watched, it moved a few steps in their direction. Now Bramble could see clearly the outline of a large owl with water dripping from its feathers. It must have landed while they were talking. His nose twitched, but he could smell only moss and wet spruce. He saw the owl scan the undergrowth as if it knew something was there, its eyes giant and pitiless; only the dark recess under their spruce tree kept them hidden. They stayed motionless—a hare's first line of defence—and Bramble whispered into Kas's ear, "Don't panic; it'll spot any movement." He knew he wasn't far from panic himself.

Suddenly, the owl spread its enormous wings and flew toward them. It landed a few feet up in their tree, and they heard it moving around: Was it coming down branch by branch? Kas let out a tiny squeal of fright. He looked at Bramble for a sign that they should run, but Bramble had his eyes closed, expecting the worst. They heard a branch shake as the owl took off, and a shower of raindrops came from above. Then, as silently as it had come, the owl melted into the forest on the far side of the clearing. They could breathe again, but it was some time before either of them stopped trembling.

Later, a roll of thunder came from over the lake, and in a lightning flash that followed, Bramble saw Kas staring out into the darkness. "The owl's gone, Kas. We'll be fine, and before long we'll be back in Alder Grove eating spring grass."

"Don't talk about food," said Kas. "What do you suppose Shiver and Misty are doing now?"

"They're huddled down, just like us, but they're sleeping." He looked toward his friend and smiled.

Kas sighed, "First night and almost caught by an owl; that can't be a good sign."

Journey *to* Hare Island

"But we weren't caught; that's a better sign." Bramble moved his feet around, made a more comfortable bed in the moss, and eventually fell asleep. Kas stayed awake for some time, listening to the wind and the rain playing their ancient song on the surrounding spruce trees.

Chapter 6
SERENA

Serena, your bright song
Overcame him,
Piercing his heart.
—Kas

The next morning the wind and rain tapered off only gradually, so it was midday before Bramble and Kas left their shelter. They took a deer path through a stand of large spruce trees and found a patch of grass on the banks of a stream. They were busy eating when Bramble saw movement on the far side of the stream; it was a female hare with beautiful greyish brown fur. He nudged Kas and pointed. Kas laughed and said, "Leave it to you to find the nearest doe, but we're supposed to avoid strangers, remember?"

The doe hopped around playfully; either she hadn't seen them or she was putting on a show.

"Hello there!" Bramble hollered.

The stranger looked startled, but quickly a shy smile lit up her face.

"Do you live around here?" asked Bramble.

"Just over there in Thornfield." She gave a sideways nod with her pretty head. "Why don't you come over here where the grass is greener?"

Journey to Hare Island

Kas shook his head, but Bramble whispered, "No harm as long as we don't get close." He jumped across the stream. Kas sat watching for a moment, looked wistfully at the trail, and then followed.

"My name is Bramble, and he's Kas. We're from Alder Grove, back along the lake. What's your name?"

"Serena. Now you two finish eating."

Kas bent down and began to eat, and Bramble joined in. When they looked full, Serena asked politely, "Would you mind helping me take some food back to Thornfield? It's not far."

"Why do you need to take food back? Is someone sick?" asked Bramble.

"Oh no," said Serena. "A friend hurt his leg and can't move very far."

Kas made motions that he and Bramble should get back on the trail.

"How about we take one bunch in and then go?" suggested Bramble.

"It would be wonderful if you could help. We could each cut off some grass ..." She stopped talking as tears welled up in her eyes.

"Come on, Kas," said Bramble, "we weren't told to be mean."

Kas sat and studied a herring gull soaring by overhead, but when Bramble and Serena each started to pile grass on the ground, he joined in. When he got close enough to Bramble, he whispered, "Those tears came pretty fast."

Not long after that, the trio followed the trail that led to Thornfield: Serena in front, followed by Bramble then Kas, all with grass sticking out the sides of their mouths. Needless to say, they didn't talk as they went along.

A layer of grey clouds still hid the sun, and the air had turned cold. They went through a patch of stunted, gnarled spruce and finally came to an expanse of wild roses, with trails here and there cutting into the bushes—this must be Thornfield. Bramble caught a faint odour on the air, like the smell of dead seaweed down by the pond, but not as pleasant. When he looked over, Kas was wrinkling his nose.

Bramble was about to tell Serena that he and Kas had to go when he suddenly stopped.

Kas put down the grass he was carrying. "What's the matter?" he asked.

Bramble dropped his grass as well. "Looks like someone is here to welcome us."

Then Kas saw, partially hidden by one of the bushes ahead, a group of five hares watching their approach.

"What is it this time, Serena?" a voice from the waiting group demanded.

Serena moved off to the side. "These are my new friends. They've been helping me, so be nice to them."

The five hares came toward the visitors. "So who are you?" the largest hare asked.

"Just travellers wanting to help," said Bramble. "We'll be on our way now."

The leader didn't sound grateful as he said, "All well and good, but you're in Thornfield territory, so you'll have to explain yourselves to our First Hare. Come with us."

"Go with them, please," said Serena. "Our First Hare is kind; you'll be allowed to stay, and we really need help."

"We can't stay, Serena," said Bramble. "We have a job of our own to do." He signalled for Kas to follow him back along the trail, but the welcoming committee was getting closer.

"That wasn't a request you can ignore," said the leader. "Take a look in back of you."

When Bramble looked, he was horrified to see hares in a big semicircle behind them: He had led Kas into a trap. He turned back to face the leader. The big hare moving toward him stumbled and raised his front paws to keep his balance. Bramble was close enough now to make out the leader's face, and what he saw horrified him: The poor creature was weeping at the corners of his eyes, and he grimaced with pain every time he took a step. Bramble glanced at the leader's four companions; they all looked ill.

The line of hares behind Kas and Bramble was also advancing, and Kas was watching them carefully as he said, "Look, they're shuffling. Some look like they died a month ago, and there's a funny smell in the air. Let's get out of here, Bram."

Bramble turned toward the path and put on a burst of speed. By changing direction every time his paws touched the ground, he eluded the advancing line and started back along the trail. When he looked behind him, he saw that a tightening circle had formed around his friend. Kas was slower than Bramble was, but he was elusive: He darted left, then turned sharply right. As Bramble watched, paws reached toward Kas from every direction, but he slipped between two surprised hares and followed Bramble up the trail.

A number of the hares set out after them, but they were lumbering and slow and soon fell behind. Just before Bramble and Kas reached the stand of spruce trees, they heard a plaintive cry from Serena: "Please come back!" Kas threw Bramble a nervous glance, but Bramble's pace didn't slow.

They moved quickly, the spruce trees a blur off to the sides, and eventually found the glade where they had gathered grass.

They sat beside the stream as their heartbeats came back to normal. Thankfully, the only scent in the air now was the salty freshness of the lake.

"What do you suppose they wanted us for?" asked Kas. "To eat us?"

"I think we'd be gathering food until we were too sick to work. Anyway, you were right about Serena, and the First Hare was right about staying away from strangers. Some leader I turned out to be."

"Listen, Bram," said Kas, "I've never seen you turn down anyone in need, and we didn't touch any of them, not even Serena."

"I'm still a dumb Swampie, but thanks." Then he shook his head, "Can you imagine Thornfield this winter? Maybe even Alder Grove? Hares with runny eyes stumbling about—is that how Thorny and Shiver will end up, Kas?"

"Don't even think about it, Bram."

Bramble closed his eyes and said, "We have a job to do, but it could have ended right here because of me." Then he stood up, kicked a nearby rock so hard he hurt his paw, grimaced, and looked toward the east. "I hope I can learn from my mistakes. Let's pick up the trail again."

They found the trail and moved on into the afternoon's growing shadows.

Chapter 7
TREAT OR TROUBLE?

One afternoon Bramble and Kas came to a clearing and saw a cluster of houses and barns, with men working in a nearby field. A large stream, crossed by a wooden bridge, ran from north to south on the other side of the buildings. The bridge could be reached only by going close to the buildings, so Bramble and Kas crouched down in a clump of hawthorn bushes to wait until nightfall, when they hoped to cross the bridge without being seen.

Darkness came, and a comforting display of stars dotted the sky. Bramble and Kas began to move quietly around the buildings but stopped when they heard voices. They peeked around the corner of the nearest barn.

Kas edged closer to Bramble. "Look at those two children coming: One looks like a little bear, and the other one is white from head to foot. We've never seen children dressing like that at home, have we?" The two children went up to one of the houses, and the hares heard a tapping sound. A door at the front of the house opened. People in the doorway laughed and looked surprised, and then they put something in the bags that the children carried. Finally, the little ones left, and the same thing happened at the next house.

"Hey look," said Kas, "that one's eating something from his bag; the people at the houses are giving out food. Here come three more children, and the smallest one's got ears like a hare. I bet they'll get food, too, and I'm hungry."

Bramble looked over at Kas and laughed. "Don't even think about it."

"Why not? The little ones have their faces covered, and some look like animals. We could stand on our hind legs, hold out our paws, and see what happens. If they chased us, we'd just run away."

Bramble hoped Kas was just teasing but said, "How do you come up with these ideas? It's a hilarious scene to imagine, but no thanks." Suddenly he poked Kas on the shoulder and pointed: A big dog had come out of one of the houses and was looking their way. "Let's get out of here," Bramble whispered. The dog jumped from the step, and the two hares bolted for the bridge. They crossed it, their feet making an exaggerated *clunk, clunk, clunk* on the wooden planking. The dog erupted into a fit of barking, but it was quite fat and gave up even before Bramble and Kas scrambled into the bushes.

They slowed down and then hid in a thick clump of wild roses. Bramble turned to his friend and said, "Kas, your stomach will get us in trouble yet."

Kas looked hurt. "Well I've got bad news; I get hungry every day, and I haven't eaten much since yesterday."

They were moving away from the settlement and around the edge of a small pond when Kas called out, "What are these? Can we eat them?" He was standing in a patch of mushrooms, a cluster of white against a background of dried grass. They did look tempting, even to Bramble. Kas looked closely at the mushrooms and said, "The first thing my mother taught me was to stay away from strange foods. Lucky she's not here." He took a nibble of the nearest mushroom and smiled, "Tastes good. Come on, Bram, this is a gift; these things should be dead by now."

Bramble sat, wondering whether he should join in. He heard a splash as a frog jumped into the pond behind him. Then he shrugged and began to eat. He had devoured four or five mushrooms when he saw Kas raise his head. "Hold on," Kas said, "I'm feeling a bit strange."

"Are you sick?"

"No, but I'm dizzy."

Bramble looked carefully at Kas and said, "Stop moving around, Kas."

"Bram, I'm standing still."

"We'd better find a place to hide," Bramble said. "I feel strange too."

They made unsteady progress away from the pond and came to a large maple tree with ferns growing around its base. Kas staggered into the ferns, flopped down, and said, "Far as I go, old friend." Bramble looked around, decided they would be hidden well enough by the ferns, and joined Kas. They lay on a thin covering of dead ferns and maple leaves. It was comfortable enough, but for a while Bramble felt the ground moving under him. Then he fell asleep.

There was mist and a light rain when Bramble opened his eyes. It was still night. He looked over and saw that Kas was sleeping. Then his eyes were drawn to a spot near the trunk of the maple and his nose twitched: He couldn't smell anything, but there was a figure standing there. "Who's there?" he called.

The figure moved closer and whispered, "Hello, Bramble. How have you been?"

"Do I know you?" asked Bramble. The hare moved closer still, and Bramble started to tremble. "It can't be you? I saw you killed by an owl." Bramble touched the scar on his cheek. "Is this a dream, Mother?"

"It's hard to explain, Bramble: *Halloween, Night of the Dead, Samhain*. Anyway, we don't have much time."

Bramble started to move closer to his mother, but she motioned him to stop. "I don't want to frighten you, dear, but we can't even touch. I'm only here to help you meet some ... individuals."

"Shouldn't we wake Kas, then?"

"Tell him about it in the morning."

Some distance from Bramble and his mother, a large man appeared in the mist. Bramble whispered, "We should run?"

"No one will hurt you tonight, Bramble. Now pay attention."

The man spoke: "The wind is fair tonight; I should go. But it's hard to go when she wants me to stay. Beautiful she is, young and supple, and I'm growing old. Choices. Decisions. Of course I'll have to go; my wife and son are waiting." He covered his face with his hands, then pulled at his greying beard, and Bramble saw a tear on his cheek.

Mother whispered to Bramble, "He's agonized like this before, but he always decides to go. He's a hero, you know, first and foremost of travellers, Ulysses himself."

"Why is he speaking hare language?" asked Bramble.

"He isn't, dear, but we just understand tonight."

"Where is he supposed to go, then?"

"On with his journey, just like you. Brave the wine-dark seas. Make his way back home, no matter what."

Bramble reached out a paw to touch his mother, but his hand felt only air. He cried out, which caught the attention of

Journey *to* Hare Island

Ulysses. "And who are you, long-eared stranger?" Ulysses asked. "A sea monster? A god in animal form? Poseidon? Speak!"

"You'd better say something," whispered Mother. "Tell him about your quest."

Bramble's voice sounded tiny in comparison with the visitor's, but he managed to say, "Well, sir, my friend and I are on a journey, a quest. We're looking for an island, but we don't know exactly where it is or what we'll find there."

"I know what you mean: one-eyed giants, sorcerers, girls. Dangerous places, islands."

Mother whispered in Bramble's ear, "Ask him what you should do."

"Sometimes we feel like giving up and going home," said Bramble meekly.

"Going home?" roared Ulysses. "You can't go home. Who ever heard of a hero going home before his task is finished? When it's finished, *then* you go home, if you can. It won't be easy, but your loved ones are waiting." Ulysses looked over at Bramble. "Aren't they?"

"The whole of Alder Grove is waiting," answered Bramble. Then he added, "But we're still not sure what we're supposed to do on the island."

"Nonsense!" said Ulysses. "What kind of hero are you? Do what you were asked to do, or you'll give us all a bad name. There may be trials and obstacles ahead, but stop whining and you'll succeed." He turned away and looked at the sky before he said, "The wind is picking up; I must go." He faded away quickly.

Mother had a reassuring look on her face. "What did I tell you? He gave you good advice. Your journey is important, Bramble, and it'll be a time of growth for you and Kas

— 33 —

if you finish it. Besides, you should enjoy the journey itself; a man called Basho once wrote, 'Every day is a journey, and the journey itself is home.'"

"Oh Mother, *Basho?* I've never heard of him. I know you want to help, but I'm just confused; this is the first journey I've ever made."

"I know you, Bramble, even though our time together was short. You'll do the right thing. And now you have only two more visitors to meet." Even as she spoke, an older man appeared. He had armour on his upper body and was leading a horse. He tried three times to mount the horse, then gave up. He turned toward Bramble and tried to look dignified as he said, "I am Don Quixote de la Mancha, knight errant, righter of wrongs, and protector of people in distress."

"Well," said Bramble, "I'm in distress and could use some advice. My friend and I are on a journey to an island, but we aren't sure where it is."

"You want directions? I don't do directions; I let my horse decide the way. Concentrate on *why* you're travelling. Do your duty to your fellow men, or rather rabbits. Don't you know why you're travelling?"

"Because I was asked to go; it's as simple as that. And I'm a hare, sir, if you don't mind. So I should do my duty and keep going. Ulysses told me the same thing."

"Ulysses!" shouted the knight. "That womanizer? Females are here to inspire you, young hare. Now I have to go and find someone else to help." He disappeared.

"Did he help me?" asked Bramble.

"Never mind," Mother said. "Here's your last visitor, Bramble. You'll be happy to know he's a lagomorph."

"A lagomorph? Are they dangerous?"

Journey *to* Hare Island

Bramble's mother laughed. "My dear, *we* are lagomorphs. Hares and rabbits are lagomorphs. And Bramble, be especially polite with this one, it's the Great Hare himself. He's sacred to the Mi'kmaq people: a creator god, a trickster, and a shape changer who can take any animal form he wants."

Bramble heard the voice before he saw the hare. "Are you progressing, young Bramble? You still have a few days to travel."

"You know who I am and where I'm going, Great Hare?"

The visitor stepped out of the mist; he was the largest hare Bramble had ever seen. "Of course I know where you're going; I know everything around these parts. You're from Alder Grove, and you're going to Hare Island."

Bramble was almost speechless, but he managed to ask, "Would you know the way to Hare Island, then?"

"Certainly. I usually give advice only to my Mi'kmaq people, but you *are* a hare. You and Kas are doing fine; continue along the lake a few more days, and you'll see Hare Island. Be careful along the way, and I'll try to keep an eye on you. Now I must go: I've got to change some weather up at Potlotek." He waved goodbye, turned, and like the others, disappeared in the mist.

"Bramble, I'm proud of you," said his mother. "Even the Great Hare knows about your journey, and he's going to keep an eye on you and Kas. I'm so glad I was allowed to see you again."

Bramble was now finding it hard to make out her features. "But Mother, do you have to go right away?" he asked. "Couldn't we talk for a while?"

"I'm afraid I do have to go. You go back to sleep." Bramble was able to keep his eyes open, but only long enough to fill with tears as the mist took his mother away again.

Chapter 8
BAGGED

One hare in a stew;
That would be too hot
Ever to let it happen,
Whether it's me or not.
—Kas

Bramble opened his eyes and looked around. Kas was asleep, but the morning sun shone through the sparse leaves of the autumn maple. Bramble hopped around the trunk of the tree: no mist and no sign of any visitors. He poked Kas on the shoulder and said, "Wake up, we have to go."

A groggy Kas tried to focus on Bramble. "What's going on?"

"It's morning. How do you feel?"

Kas got up and stretched. "Not too steady, but I'm okay."

They sat under the tree, squinting in the bright sunlight. A raven croaked on a branch way above them, and Kas jumped up when a garter snake slithered by, almost at their feet.

"Kas, did you hear anything during the night?" Bramble asked.

Kas looked over at Bramble and said, "Did a herd of coyotes stop for a chat? No, I didn't hear anything."

Bramble knew his story would sound bizarre but decided to tell it anyway. "I had a sort of adventure last night; it could have been a dream. Anyway, right here under the tree, I met some individuals, including the Great Hare, a big snowshoe hare. You'll never guess who introduced them to me?"

Kas looked at the maple tree and said, "Surprise me."

"My mother."

"Bramble," said Kas, "you ate mushrooms. You zonked out. You were asleep. You and I both know your mother is dead."

"I know all that, Kas, but it happened right here. There was mist and rain, but I saw everything clearly."

Kas smiled. "Bram, look at the ground. What do you notice?"

"What?"

"It's dry; it couldn't have rained last night."

Bramble stared at the ground; it was certainly dry. If it was all a dream, the rest of the story could wait. "Mother?" he whispered to himself. Then he got up and said abruptly, "Okay, let's look for some food and then find the trail." He hoped he sounded more confident than he felt.

The day was bright but cool—a good day to make up time. They found the main trail leading east. It was narrow but straight, so they moved quickly. Bramble sniffed at the path and said, "I smell humans; if we see any, we'll find a route closer to the shore."

By midday, they were going through hardwoods, with some red and yellow leaves still on the trees. At one point, they startled a pair of ruffed grouse that whirred off through the undergrowth, and every so often, they surprised mice that scampered from the trail. Crows passed overhead, along with an occasional herring gull, but there were no hawks or eagles. Later the path led back into spruce and fir trees.

Bramble felt something hard glance off his shoulder and fall to the path behind him. He turned to shout a warning, but before he could, Kas cried, "Hey, let go of my leg! Something's got my leg!" He tried hard to pull his leg away but couldn't.

"Stop pulling while I take a look," said Bramble. "There's a loop of something around your leg, and it's attached to a tree by a vine. I'll chew through the vine." After he tried, Bramble yelped, "I almost broke a tooth. That vine's too hard, and the loop tightens when you pull, so don't pull. It must be what the seniors call a *snare*."

Kas looked mournfully at Bramble and said, "Some owl or coyote will find me."

"There must be something we can do."

"Look," said Kas, "if anything comes, you have a job to do, so get out of here."

Both hares froze when they heard movement in a clump of dead ferns near the path, but it was only a flicker scratching for food, and it soon flew away. They sat there and tried to think. Bramble was staring down the path to the east when he saw movement in the distance, and his heart jumped. It was two humans, a man and a boy. Kas shook with fright and whispered, "I'm dead, Bram; they'll kill me."

Bramble watched the humans for a moment, then turned to Kas. "I won't desert you, I promise, but the only thing I can do for now is hide and watch. I can't fight humans." Kas nodded in sad agreement. Bramble hopped into some nearby bushes while Kas made a futile attempt to sink into the short grass of the path.

Journey *to* Hare Island

The man had two dead hares slung over his shoulder. Bramble shuddered; would Kas join them? As the humans came close, the boy moved ahead. He pointed to a bag the man was carrying and pleaded for something. They watched for a moment. Then the man reached down and grabbed Kas by the back of the neck. Kas squealed, but the man pulled the loop from around his leg and stuffed him, alive and squirming, into the bag. He placed the snare again so that it dangled just above the path, and then the two turned and went back the way they had come, the bag cradled in the boy's arms.

When they were far enough away, Bramble came out of hiding. He made a wide circle around the snare and followed them down the path.

It was now evening, so when the humans left the main path and headed inland, Bramble moved closer to keep them in sight. He had no idea where they were going or how to help Kas, but, as promised, he kept following. Spruce and fir branches reached from trees on either side, forming a roof over the path. The scent of the evergreens was sharp, almost painful, in Bramble's nostrils.

Eventually the forest gave way to a clearing, with a house in the centre and a small barn off to the side. The humans headed for the barn and entered by a door that faced the house. Bramble watched from the bushes. After a short time, they left the barn and went to the house. A dog came bounding down the steps, circled the clearing, sniffed at the front of the barn, and then was let back into the house. A short while later, the boy carried something out and left it in the barn.

Bramble's heart was pounding, but he waited, crouching down in the protection of some alders, until no sounds were coming from the house. It was well into the night when he crept from the bushes. Moonlight glinted off the house and barn, making Bramble even more cautious. He circled the barn quietly but could find no way in. A crack between two boards let him peep inside, but all was dark and quiet. He put an ear to the crack and listened: nothing. He sniffed and confirmed that Kas was somewhere near. After a nervous glance toward the house, he whispered through the crack, "Kas!" No answer. He tried again, a bit louder: "Kas, are you there?"

"Bramble?"

"Are you tied up or what?"

"Remember the *cage* they sometimes had the dog in at home? I'm in one of those."

"I saw the boy bring something out to the barn. What was it?"

"Some carrots and other things, but he made sure I couldn't get out when he opened the cage door. I think he wants to keep me or fatten me up to eat."

"Kas, I don't really think they're worried about fattening you up." Bramble heard nervous laughter from the barn. "Okay. Listen, Kas, I'll watch my chance when he brings you food. I'll surprise him when he opens the cage door, and you try to escape. Then we'll both have to scram; there's a big dog in the house."

"Bram, I want to get out, but will that plan work?"

"I don't have any other ideas, Kas. I'll be watching. You be ready to move."

Early the next morning, the boy came from the house and entered the barn. Bramble made his way quietly to the door.

Journey *to* Hare Island

He heard the boy talking to Kas and then a squeak as the cage door opened. It was time, but at that critical moment, the door of the house banged behind him. When he glanced over his shoulder, the dog was on the step, looking directly at him. Bramble rounded the corner of the barn and made for the bushes. He risked a glance over his shoulder when he was entering the bushes and was relieved to see that the dog had followed but was falling behind. He hadn't gone too far into the bushes when his ears told him the dog had given up. Bramble was safe for now, but Kas was still a captive.

Much later, Bramble made his way back to the side of the barn. He whispered through the crack, "Kas, I'll try again tomorrow."

"I thought maybe that dog got you."

"No chance; we can both outrun him. Let's hope the boy thinks the dog was chasing a bird; I don't think he saw me."

Bramble knew there was only a slim chance he could free Kas, but he tried to sound confident as he continued, "You be ready, Kas; I won't give up."

Early the next morning, the boy once again entered the barn, and Bramble positioned himself near the door. The dog was nowhere in sight. As soon as the boy opened the cage, Bramble made a wild rush into the barn and crossed in front of the boy. Then he hopped around in circles, trying to keep the boy's attention. He yelled, "Go Kas!"

Kas began to move, but the boy noticed and slammed the cage door. Bramble grew desperate. He moved to the side of the cage and said, "I'm not leaving, Kas, I don't care what he does."

The boy closed the barn door, then changed his mind and opened it again. He found a long piece of wood leaning against the wall and tried to chase Bramble out of the building. Kas screamed, "Get out, Bram, get out!" But Bramble wouldn't listen; he continued to avoid the stick and always went back to the side of the cage. The boy finally shook his head and stood looking at the two hares. He opened the door of the cage and left the barn. Kas came out of the cage cautiously, and the two hares moved to the door, expecting to be struck with something or have the dog attack them. No dog. The boy was sitting on the steps of the house, watching them. They broke for the bushes. When Bramble looked back, the boy was still sitting there. "He's not chasing us," Bramble said in disbelief. "He let us go."

After they reached the protection of the bushes and Kas caught his breath, he said simply, "I think he knows you're my friend."

Chapter 9
DUSTY

Each day Bramble and Kas went to the shore to see if Hare Island was in sight, but they were always disappointed. Then one morning when the sun had melted the night's frost, they stood on a low headland. Below them small waves swished against a rocky shoreline. They looked east, stared, and Kas finally broke the silence: "Do I see what I think I see?"

Bramble was quiet. East of them was a large island with a hill on its western end. At last he said, "It's a couple of days up the shore, but it's there." And then, before he could help himself, he added, "The Great Hare was right."

"Dreaming again?" asked Kas. He poked Bramble playfully on the shoulder, and they started back inland to find the trail.

In the afternoon they came across a clearing with grass showing above a thin layer of snow. "It's getting colder every day," said Kas. "We should enjoy this while we can."

They were happily chomping on the grass when an angry voice said from close by, "Leapin' leverets, eating my grass. Want me to starve?"

They were startled. When they looked around they saw, partly hidden under a spruce bough, an odd-looking hare: His left ear was upright, but his right hung limply down the side of his head, and his fur was in patches of white and brown.

"We have to eat somewhere," said Bramble. "You can't eat all this before it's buried, can you?"

"Probably not," said the stranger, "but you could ask." He hopped out into the open and sat near Bramble and Kas. "My winter coat came early, so I look a mess, don't I?"

"No problem," said Kas, "we've started, too." He held up a hind paw that was almost completely white and pointed to a patch on Bramble's shoulder. "We didn't know anyone lived here. May we please have some grass?"

"Who said I live here? I only eat here. Help yourself."

Bramble told the stranger their names and added, "We're from Alder Grove, and we have to get to that island." He pointed toward the lake.

The strange hare sat up. "Hope you don't mean Hare Island?"

"Why not?" asked Bramble.

"Hard to get to, and they don't like visitors. Why go there anyway?"

Kas looked toward Bramble but said to the stranger, "We were told to go there by our First Hare, but he was weak on reasons."

Bramble added quickly, "We have to get something there for home. We don't know many details, but we trust our First Hare."

"Well, eat and then we'll see about Hare Island. Name's Dusty, by the way."

After they ate, they sat under a fir tree near the lake, where they could look out but were hidden from eagles or hawks cruising the beach. A raft of eider ducks floated offshore, and beyond them was a scattering of seagulls. The mist-covered hills on the far side of the lake made a perfect backdrop. The lake wasn't as wide here, but Hare Island, looking green and peaceful, was still a long distance away.

"I live inland a bit," said Dusty.

Bramble asked politely, "You haven't seen any disease in your district lately, have you?"

"Not a sneeze, but we hear there's sickness farther west." His look said he expected a response.

"Oh no, we're perfectly healthy," said Bramble.

Dusty seemed satisfied and went on," Now, getting to Hare Island? You could swim, but you'd freeze your bum if you tried now. In two months you can cross on the ice; that's your best bet."

"We have to go now," said Bramble.

"Then there's only one way I can suggest: Find a big branch or a tree trunk on the shore, one that floats stable; wait till the wind's aimed at the Island, jump on, and hope for the best. It's been done. I'll show you a point of land that's got driftwood."

Kas wasn't very encouraged. "So it's a miserable place?"

"I hear it's a nice place; it's just hard to get to and mean to strangers. Got to get home soon, so let's go. I'll take you halfway, but you'll find the point from there. Of course you'll have to cross Big Swamp." He studied their faces to see if they knew about the swamp.

"Big Swamp?" asked Bramble.

"Don't know Big Swamp? Ponds and marshes from the lake to way inland."

"Is it frozen over yet?" asked Bramble.

"Some; it's cold these nights, but you'll have to take care. Wait till the morning to cross so you can see where you're going. Now let's travel."

Kas exchanged a look with Bramble and rolled his eyes, but the two friends followed Dusty into a dense fir and spruce forest. They saw only one other animal on their way, a deer that stood by the path calmly and watched them as they went by. In late afternoon they left the evergreens and entered a stretch of hardwoods, then some alders and small willows, and finally Big Swamp opened out before them. They could see patches of water where streamlets made their way toward the lake. Here and there, brownish grey bushes stood out against a thin layer of snow. A line of tall trees marked the far side.

Dusty sat on his haunches and said, "Far as I go. Keep a straightish line to the trees, then follow the edge of the swamp to the point. Pray it doesn't snow and hide things. Good luck." They watched him make his way back along the path, his right ear dangling against the side of his head.

"I don't know about this, Bram," said Kas. "We can be careful and get across the swamp, but that floating log idea? Maybe he just thought it up?"

Bramble picked at some cranberry plants with a front paw and answered, "Could be, Kas, but what else can we do? Our friends back home are in more danger than we are." He settled down into the moss. "We'll feel better after some rest." They stared out at Big Swamp, where a hawk swooped and hovered its way toward the lake. As the evening got darker, the swamp faded into a dull grey and then disappeared completely.

Chapter 10
BIG SWAMP

Alone in winter.
Only one colour
And the sound of wind.
—Basho

The next morning, after eating a hasty breakfast, Bramble and Kas made their way into the swampland. It was slow going, but at least it hadn't snowed. All morning they circled ice-covered ponds, and when they came to streamlets, they moved upstream or downstream until they could jump across.

At midday the trees on the far side still seemed distant. Kas hollered to Bramble, who was leading the way, "That snared leg is hurting, Bram."

Bramble let Kas go ahead and said, "You set a comfortable pace; I'll be right behind you." They were both tiring, but they were hoping to reach the other side before evening, so now they started crossing some of the ice-covered ponds.

The sky turned grey, and in the afternoon it began to snow. With their large back paws, Bramble and Kas could handle snow better than most animals, but on Big Swamp visibility was very important. They struggled on. It grew even colder, and the wind picked up, sending stinging blasts of snow into their faces.

"Will we find shelter soon?" asked Kas. "My leg is getting stiff."

Bramble looked around and said, "Looks like a clump of bushes on the other side of this pond. The ice looks solid, so I'm going to cross; stay here until I reach the other side. Once you start over, keep moving."

When Bramble got most of the way across, he turned to tell Kas to follow, but at that moment he heard ice cracking under his paws. He tried to jump clear, but the ice gave way and he felt the shock of frigid water. Like all hares Bramble could swim, but when he surfaced and tried to climb onto the thin ice, it broke under his weight. His limbs grew stiff, but he kept pawing at the ice in front of him to scramble up. He was sinking lower with each thrust and, at one point, took a big gulp of freezing water.

He was about ready to give up when he realized that the edge of the pond was close. If he could break enough ice, he might reach the shore. He attacked the ice as fiercely as his stiffening body would allow, using his weight to force his way through. He was struggling for breath when he finally touched the bottom and, with a lunge, reached the shore.

His sense of relief was short-lived: He was now at the mercy of wet fur, freezing temperatures, and strong wind. He looked around frantically for Kas, afraid that he, too, had gone through the ice, but there he was, coming around the end of the pond.

"Bram, are you okay? I saw you go through the ice. How did you get out?"

"I'll tell you later. I'm soaked. I'll freeze with this wind."

When Kas turned, he saw the clump of bushes just ahead. "Can you make it over there?"

With his friend's help, Bramble struggled toward the bushes. "Wind's too much for me," he said. "I can't make it."

"Yes, you can. We're almost there. I'll see if there's enough shelter in the middle." Kas pushed into the bushes but came back out in panic. "There's a big animal lying down in there, and I didn't stay around to see what it was. We'll have to find another place."

Bramble gasped for breath before he said, "I'll freeze." He crept into the bushes, and Kas could only follow. Three stunted spruce trees grew in a clump, with wild rose bushes around their base. Snow caught by the bushes created a small open area. Something alive lay on the far side, its back to them. The animal lifted its head. With relief they saw it was an adult deer.

Bramble dropped not far from the deer, chilled to the bone. He whimpered a few times and then lapsed into sleep. Kas fought exhaustion, concerned for Bramble, but was soon asleep as well.

During the night Kas woke and looked around. Survival had won out over Bramble's other instincts; his friend was stretched out alongside the sleeping deer, seeking its warmth.

Bramble could feel the warmth of the deer's body, but ice still gripped his insides. He was losing his will to survive. "I can't make it," he thought. "I don't want to go on. Please let me die."

A voice scolded him, "Why would you say that? You've faced other challenges. Why give up now in sight of Hare Island?"

Bramble stirred. "I'm not strong enough. Tell them to find someone confident and strong."

He heard quiet laughter. "And where will they find such a hero? You agreed to come."

"I was given little choice."

"You agreed. Do what has to be done."

— 49 —

"I've heard that before, but I'm cold, and I feel my strength going."

"There is nothing going except your courage. Do you want to creep home and have to live in the shadows? Sleep and you'll awaken with fire and not ice in your heart."

Morning found its way into the clearing as small pillars of light. Kas awoke and shook Bramble in panic as he asked, "Bramble, are you okay?"

Bramble opened his eyes. "I was before you attacked me," he said. He looked around and stretched. "Where's the deer?" There was a flattened area on the moss next to them, but the deer was gone.

Kas hopped around anxiously in front of Bramble. "The wind is down, and I think it's stopped snowing. Come and we'll look outside."

They left their refuge and surveyed the expanse of swampland they still had to cross. Sadly, the previous day's snow had covered any signs of a safe way forward. Bramble stretched his limbs again; his strength was returning, but he knew he wouldn't survive another plunge through the ice, so he was afraid to set out blindly over the snow. Kas moved nervously back and forth in front of the bushes, then stopped and stamped his hind feet in excitement. "Look over here, Bram."

Bramble stared at the snow in front of Kas: deer tracks, clearly visible and heading east across Big Swamp. Without hesitation, they began following the tracks. The deer seemed to know the way, and any ice it crossed would be solid enough for snowshoe hares. They made slow but steady progress, and by midday they were safely into the trees.

Journey *to* Hare Island

When Kas looked around to see where the deer had gone, he could find no deer tracks. "The only thing I see are tracks of a big snowshoe hare," he said.

As Dusty had suggested, they followed the edge of the swamp all the way to the lake, and by dusk they were bedded down near the launching point. The sky was still dull, and Hare Island looked ominous across a choppy lake. "I hope the wind is down some by morning," said Bramble.

Bramble and Kas sat lost in their own thoughts for a time, but then Bramble asked in a serious tone, "Kas, did I talk to you last night after we settled down?"

"Are you kidding? You couldn't keep your eyes open. You must have been dreaming again."

"I guess so," said Bramble. He was quiet for a while, then he said, "Kas, don't you find it odd that the deer kept me warm, and then made tracks that led us in exactly the right direction?"

Kas smiled. "Sure, maybe it was the deer you were talking to."

"And maybe I'll dream again tonight," said Bramble.

"Wouldn't hurt a bit," said Kas. "Talk to some fish; we might need them tomorrow."

Chapter 11
ADRIFT

There is no path on lake waters;
Only a hope for what's ahead.
And there could be dragons.
—*Kas*

Early the next morning, Bramble and Kas began searching the shore for a large piece of driftwood, disturbing a blue heron that flapped away with an angry squawk. The sky was clear, and luckily the wind was blowing gently toward Hare Island.

"Here's one," said Bramble. The log was already half in the water. He and Kas pushed on the shore end until the log was afloat. They jumped to the top and sat, but the log rolled suddenly and they landed in the water. Kas muttered as they waded to shore.

They found a second log with a few small branches at one end and one large branch halfway up the trunk. They pushed and pulled until it could float. When they jumped onto the log, the large branch lay on one side in the water, and their craft sat steadily in its place. "Don't think I could have pushed another one," said Kas. "Let's sit for a while." They pulled it back until it touched the bottom, then they sat together on the shore to dry off.

Journey *to* Hare Island

A loon cried way out on the lake. Kas groaned, "You know what that means?"

"I remember what the old ones say," said Bramble. "Loons call to hares long dead. But we're not dead."

"They must be practicing," said Kas. Then he stood up and asked, "Well, are we crazy enough to try this?"

"With the right wind, it's now or never."

"Once we leave shore, it's all luck," said Kas. "We hit the Island, or we go sailing off into the lake." Then with a sigh, he pushed hard on one end of the log, and Bramble pushed on the other end. They soon had the log afloat, though they got wet again in the process. They both settled down toward the centre and waited. The log scraped bottom twice, then was free. They crouched lower as small waves rocked the log gently. Slowly they drifted away from the land.

By the middle of the afternoon, they were halfway across. The wind had shifted slightly toward the west, but it remained steady.

"I shouldn't mention it," said Kas, "but we haven't seen an eagle." Because their fur was now partly white, they could be spotted easily from above, but only a herring gull had soared close to inspect their craft.

Suddenly, Bramble sat upright and looked around. "What's that sound?" A roar came from farther east on the lake. "I see it," Bramble said. "It looks tiny from here, but it's getting bigger. It's coming this way."

"I see it, too," said Kas, "It's a boat like we see off Alder Grove, but it's turning away."

They settled down, but Bramble was back up almost immediately. "It's turned back this way. I see it better now. It's coming fast, and it isn't small."

— 53 —

"What if humans are coming to kill us?"

"They wouldn't be out here looking for hares, but I hope they see this log."

Both of them were trembling as the boat came straight at them. Their ear openings were flat against their heads in a failing attempt to block out the painful sound. There was nowhere to run and nothing they could do. "Two humans in the boat, and they're looking at the shore!" shouted Bramble. "If they don't look this way soon, we're dead!"

"Should we jump?" Kas hollered.

"Too far to swim; hold on!"

The boat was a monster towering over them when it made a sudden turn to the north. The log, struck by a powerful wave, lurched sideways and almost broke free of the water before plunging back, submerging, and then settling into its original position.

Both hares were washed from the log. Bramble was thrown against the side branch and then back toward the centre, where he managed to hold on. Kas was swept off the log, which struck him a glancing blow as it settled back into the water. When Bramble looked, Kas was floating beside the log, his head submerged. The wind was still pushing the log toward the north; Kas could be left behind.

Bramble didn't hesitate. He jumped into the water and pushed Kas toward the tree, hoping they could use footholds on the small branches near the end to get back on. He managed to drape Kas over one of the branches, making sure his head was clear of the water. He found leverage with his own hind feet on another branch and pushed himself up onto the log. Kas was sputtering and coughing, but at least he was alive. He struggled to his feet, looking dazed for a few minutes before he turned to Bramble and asked, "What happened? Where's the boat?"

"It kept going down the lake. Are you okay now?"

"My head hurts, and I'm full of salt water. Ugh!"

"Hare Island's getting closer," said Bramble. "Let's hope we can land without needing to swim. You sit there and clear your head."

Later Bramble again checked their position. He studied the waters around the log and said, "I think the wind's shifted even farther toward the west; we're drifting along the shore." They both watched anxiously, and finally it was obvious that they might miss even the western point and drift on into the lake.

"That's it; we'll have to swim," Bramble told Kas. "No thinking—you go first. I'll go right behind you and keep you in sight."

Kas moved to the front of the log and jumped as far toward the shore as he could. Bramble followed, went under for a moment, and then came to the surface. He was coughing but swimming hard. They were low in the water so the wind wasn't pushing them farther west, but they rose and fell as waves hit them at an angle from behind.

Every time he was lifted by a wave, Bramble could see Kas swimming strongly. The shore was close now, and Bramble knew he should soon touch bottom. There it was: a momentary bump as he fell into the trough of a wave, and then firm bottom with the next trough. He pushed himself through the surf, and when he reached a firm footing, he looked to make sure Kas had also reached safety. There he was, sitting farther up from the water and looking directly at Bramble. Kas waved a paw and said something. What Bramble heard was mostly sputtering, but he thought he knew what Kas was trying to say: "Welcome to Hare Island."

Chapter 12
RECEPTION

A sprinkling of snow covered the wide upper beach. The plants and trees looked familiar: beach peas, grass, and bayberry led to a band of maple and yellow birch, with spruce and fir even farther back. Bramble turned to Kas and said, "So we're on Hare Island; now let's find the locals."

Kas was still sitting on the beach. "Why such a hurry?"

"We can't hide on a strange island," said Bramble. "This is the western end, so let's go around the point and head east on the far shore. If we stick close to the water, we won't have to climb that hill." He pointed to the cliff rising steeply from the western tip.

Kas got up and shook water from his fur. Thankfully, the bright sun would dry them quickly. They started west, following the shoreline but keeping close to the trees in case they saw predators. They were skirting the inner edge of a small pond when Bramble stopped and his nose twitched before he said, "There's a snowshoe hare not far away." He had hardly gotten the words out when a large hare jumped from the woods and stood in their path.

"Who are you?" asked the stranger in a stern voice.

Bramble tried to sound friendly as he said, "Hello there. We were hoping to meet someone."

The hare was big and rough looking, but with a spark of intelligence in his eyes. His back legs were powerful, as though he did a lot of running, and in general, he looked like a hare who would give commands and probably be obeyed. When Bramble and Kas moved toward him, he said in a loud voice, "Don't come any closer. Who gave you permission to land here?"

"We're not here to do any harm," said Bramble. "Could you take us to your First Hare?"

The stranger guffawed. "Just like that? You land uninvited and expect to be taken to the First Hare? How's that for nerve?" His last comment was directed behind Bramble and Kas; when they looked, they saw that three more hares had come out of the woods.

The hare in front spoke again: "Come with us." When he saw Bramble lift his chin and stay where he was, he added, "Or go back into the lake. Take your pick."

"We'll be telling your First Hare about this welcome," said Bramble.

This time all four Island hares laughed, and the leader said, "I'm sure my father will be happy to listen. Now follow me, but don't get too close."

As they started out, Kas mumbled, "Dusty was right; they think we're sick."

A moss-covered path led into the trees and then eastward. They trudged half the length of the Island before they stopped. A few times on the way, their noses told them there were other hares near, but they saw only a few squirrels and blue jays, all scolding them from nearby trees. When they stopped, the leader gestured and said, "Come over here." As Bramble and Kas came closer, he moved aside and directed, "See that opening between those rocks? Follow that in. There's a spring in there, and someone will bring food. That's your home until you're told otherwise." The three hares in back moved closer.

"Okay, but promise this is only temporary," said Bramble.

The leader snickered and said, "We don't promise anything; just move."

Bramble and Kas found themselves in a natural enclosure surrounded by rock walls that were much too steep to climb. They stood quietly as their eyes adjusted to the shadows. The enclosure was only a few hops wide and about the same deep. Off to the corner was a small pool of water. They heard a large stone being rolled into the entrance and more stones being placed against the first one.

"Well, that's that; we're in here forever," said a dejected Kas.

"At least we're on the Island," said Bramble. "We may not be in here long."

It was evening when they heard a sound from above. A head appeared at the edge of the rock face, and a stranger's voice yelled down, "Watch out, I've got some food." They heard something hit the floor.

"Hey, what's your name?" Bramble shouted.

"Name's Denny," said the visitor, "but I can't tell you anything."

"Why not?" asked Kas.

"I don't know, but I don't want to make Tuagh angry. I guess you'll be here until they know you're not sick."

"Who's Tuagh, and what sickness are you talking about?" asked Bramble.

"Tuagh captured you, and the sickness is the one they get on the mainland. I'll be back tomorrow morning."

"Wait," said Bramble, "How far is it to where you live?" There was no response.

They ate dried grass and drank water from the pool, which thankfully was clean and free of ice.

"Now what?" asked Kas. "Do we just sit here and bore each other, or try to find a way out?"

"Sadly, it's their rules until they know we're harmless."

Kas looked up at the rock wall and said, "If an owl or hawk sees us here, we'll be in trouble; there's nowhere to hide." He circled the enclosure, registering all the scents his nose could detect. "At least there's no sign of foxes or coyotes."

It had been a hard day from the time they pushed the logs out in the morning to their final swim to the beach. They had no trouble falling asleep.

Bramble and Kas awoke to the sound of more food hitting the floor. This time they saw no one and received no answer when they hollered. Most days that followed, early morning shadows gave way to bright sunshine, the sunshine gave way quickly to afternoon shadows because of the rock wall, and then came long evenings and nights. A few times it darkened and they knew it was snowing, although little snow made its way into their enclosure. Once in the afternoon, the shadow of a large bird crossed from one side to the other of their clearing; they crouched in fear, but the bird moved on. "Probably only a gull anyway," said the hopeful Kas. The only actual visitors were occasional chickadees coming to drink at the spring.

They studied the rock walls surrounding them, but aside from a few patches of green moss and water seeping from cracks, they presented nothing but a uniform greyness. Most of the time, they sat and talked about Alder Grove. Then one afternoon shadows moved, and when they looked up, a hare was standing near the top edge of the wall. "Is that you, Denny?" asked Bramble.

But their visitor spoke with the deep voice of an older hare. "Where are you from, and why have you come, uninvited, to our Island?"

Kas looked toward Bramble, and Bramble said, "We're from Alder Grove. Our First Hare asked us to travel here. He wants us to meet with your First Hare and get something to bring home."

They waited for a response. When it came, it was laced with anger: "That doesn't answer many questions. I've never heard of Alder Grove, and I have no idea what you could bring from here. Because of our isolation, sickness never comes here, and we want things to stay that way. My name is Antun. I was asked to advise our First Hare about you. If I have my way, you'll soon be gone."

Bramble and Kas sat looking up at the visitor. After a long pause, Antun spoke again: "You will spend three more days here. If you show no signs of illness by that time, you'll appear before a group of seniors, and they will decide what to do with you. Do you understand?"

"Yes," said two meek voices from below.

Three more anxious days passed for Bramble and Kas. They spent their time discussing questions they could be asked and trying to come up with answers. Given the attitude of Island hares they had already met, Tuagh and Antun especially, they weren't hopeful about their prospects.

Chapter 13
JUDGEMENT DAY

Finally one morning the stones were rolled back, and Tuagh stood in the entrance. "Let's get this over with," he said. "You two come with us, and don't do anything funny."

Bramble and Kas offered no resistance; they were happy to be leaving their prison at last. They followed Tuagh toward the east, once again with three large hares guarding the rear. There was snow on the trail, and the evergreens that lined the way carried patches of white. They reached an area of smaller trees and bushes: willows, aspen, and then the familiar alders and wild roses. At one point, the friends looked at each other when they spotted the tracks of a weasel that had crossed the trail, but the faint scent told them that the weasel itself had gone some time ago. They started to see other hares beside the trail, but these hares moved farther in under the bushes when they saw Bramble and Kas. "Do you see that?" whispered Kas. "They still think we'll infect them with something."

Bramble didn't respond; his mind was on the ordeal ahead.

Finally Tuagh stopped and turned to the prisoners to say, "You wait here." He went north on a side trail. Kas amused himself by glaring at their three guards.

Tuagh emerged from the bushes and motioned to the prisoners. They followed him into a large clearing ringed with spruce. Tuagh had them sit facing five older hares who formed a line in front. A large hare in the middle of the group said, "I am First Hare. Tuagh tells us he captured you sneaking onto our Island. There is sickness on the mainland, so you could be endangering us. Why did you come here?" He stopped speaking and stared first at Kas, and then at Bramble.

Bramble stood. "We have travelled a long distance and faced many difficulties. We arrived here not in secret but openly, planning to seek your help. Before we left our home, we saw only one hare who was sick, and we had no direct contact with her."

The old hare said angrily, "You see! There was sickness, and you could have brought it with you. What do you want from us anyway?"

Bramble stood taller in the face of the harsh words. "Our First Hare spoke highly of Hare Island. He thought you would have something to give us."

The seniors looked at one another, but no one spoke for several moments. Then the First Hare gestured to a young hare standing on the edge of the clearing and instructed, "Go to Wildwood and ask Rowan to come here." The hare left immediately, and the leader looked back at Kas and Bramble. "Rowan is our healer; he will know if you are free of disease. We don't want to be inhospitable, but our own health and safety must be our first concern. Tuagh, do you have anything to add?"

Tuagh took a step forward, a scowl on his face. "We are a small number living on a small island. If disease struck, we could be wiped out. We owe nothing to this Alder Grove, wherever it is. My group spends a great deal of time guarding the Island, as you know, and we don't want our efforts to be wasted." Bramble's jaw tightened; Tuagh was convincing, and Bramble saw two of the seniors nod in agreement.

Time passed in silence until a hare entered from the northern edge of the clearing. He was old, with shaggy white fur, but his eyes were bright and alert. He moved out slowly and stood between the seniors and the two strangers. He exchanged nods with some of the seniors and then addressed their leader: "Someone needs me, First Hare?"

"Greetings, Rowan. These two mainland hares were captured nine days ago and have been kept in isolation ever since. They come from a place called Alder Grove, and they admitted they had seen a sick hare before they left. If they show any signs of illness, they must be sent away immediately." He hesitated before he went on, and Bramble moved uncomfortably in his place. The First Hare continued, "They also say they were sent here to get something to take home, I suppose having to do with the illness. Does all that make sense to you?"

The healer turned and walked around the two captives. He asked Bramble to open his mouth and peered in, then poked Kas's stomach with a paw. Before he turned back to the seniors, he directed a kindly smile at both. "These are both healthy-looking hares. If they've been in isolation for nine days, there is no danger to us. I'd have to think about what we could give them to take home."

Bramble took his first deep breath in some time, but then Tuagh asked angrily, "How can you be sure they aren't sick?"

The healer's eyes opened wide. He glared at Tuagh and said, "Have you become a healer now, too?" He turned to the First Hare and his companions. "If you like, I'll take these two youngsters to Wildwood and observe them for a few more days, but we have nothing to worry about."

All the seniors stood and the First Hare said, "We'll be back shortly with our decision."

Bramble heard a buzz around the edges of the clearing when they left. A surprising number had come to see the questioning, perhaps most of the community. Tuagh and his friends grumbled amongst themselves in the centre, but Rowan now seemed relaxed and, Bramble hoped, confident.

Quiet returned when the seniors, moving slowly because two of them were very old, once again took their places. The First Hare spoke: "This has not been an easy decision. We need to protect ourselves against disease, but there is also an enduring hare tradition of sanctuary." Hardly a breath was taken in the clearing as listeners waited for the next statement. "If Rowan is able to host the two, not just for the few days he mentioned, but until they can return to the mainland, we will give them permission to stay. Further, if he is able to give them something useful to bring back to their home, we have no problem with that, either."

As soon as the First Hare finished speaking, Tuagh stepped forward. "Father, I must object. This decision ignores practices that we have followed for years." There was a thumping of agreement by hares around Tuagh.

The First Hare responded quickly, "We understand, Tuagh, but we have the final say in these matters and will not reconsider. We put great faith in the wisdom and knowledge of our healer. Visitors, do not make us regret our decision." He turned to the healer and asked, "Is it asking too much of you to host them, Rowan?"

Rowan bowed regally to the seniors. "My concern is the welfare of our hares; I know you share that concern.

— 66 —

With your permission, I will take our guests to Wildwood right away."

The First Hare nodded his assent. As Bramble and Kas were led from the clearing, Bramble looked over and was not surprised to see an angry stare coming from Tuagh, whose ears were pointing as straight as daggers along his back.

Chapter 14
WILDWOOD INTERVAL

I hear the music
Of the forest glade.
I can dance on the snow.
—Kas

Rowan, with Bramble and Kas following, crossed a large east/west trail and continued north on a smaller one. For a short distance, they saw paths leading off the trail in various directions and occasionally passed other hares, who always greeted Rowan with respect. The small paths died out, but the trail continued on; Rowan lived apart from the other hares. "Not far now," the old hare said, and shortly the trail came to an end at a low ridge topped with beach grass. "Here we are, Wildwood. Just over that ridge is the lake." Sure enough, when the two youngsters tested the air, the familiar salty smell was strong.

On the east side of the trail, just where it ended, was an opening leading into a clump of bayberry bushes. When Kas and Bramble followed Rowan in, they found a good-sized clearing, with the ridge on the lake side cut away, forming an overhang that gave protection from the weather. Little snow had made it through the thick shrubbery, and beneath the overhang the ground was dry. Here and there, in small alcoves in the bank, were piles of plants.

"Sorry about the clutter," said the old hare, "but a healer needs his medicines. As you heard, my name is Rowan, and I gather you are Kas and Bramble. I know where Alder Grove is, by the way; I was quite a traveller in my youth."

He gave them forms close to each other but well away from his own. "You can talk away," he explained, "and you won't disturb an old hare's daydreaming, or his sleep." The overhang above their forms would keep them dry in rain or snow, and the thick layer of moss on the ground would be comfortable.

"Did Tuagh arrange for you to eat this morning?" Rowan asked.

"We haven't eaten all day," said Kas.

"I can't understand that hare," said Rowan. "His father is an excellent First Hare. Come and I'll show you some seedlings. No one comes all the way out here to eat." He led them a short distance back down the trail and then west into a grove of young hardwoods. As they ate, chewing the green bark off larger twigs and eating smaller ones whole, only a red squirrel noted their presence.

"Does it get lonely out here, Rowan?" Bramble asked.

"I'll enjoy having you two for the winter—it'll civilize me a bit—but I don't mind living alone. As a young healer, I spent time gathering things by myself and enjoyed it. I had time to think." He laughed. "I'm part of the scenery out here now."

Several days later, Bramble and Rowan sat together enjoying the seedlings. Kas was a short distance away, poking around in a patch of smaller plants. Kas turned to Rowan and asked, "Which of these can you use for healing?"

Rowan hopped over and pointed out some that were useful. "I often go further afield," he said, "but there are a good number close at hand."

That afternoon they had a visit from Bayberry, one of Rowan's oldest friends. He brought ingredients for Rowan that he had gathered around his home at the east end of the Island. Kas was happy to nose around those new things as well.

"Bring Kas and Bramble down to Waterside whenever you'd like," said Bayberry. "They can look out to the mainland from there and meet Dawn."

After his friend left, Rowan explained, "Dawn is Bayberry's daughter. When her mother was taken by a coyote, he took over and made sure she survived, something not many bucks would do. She's well liked, but Tuagh has his eye on her. I don't think Bayberry is happy about that, but it's not our problem, of course."

While Bramble and Kas were getting to know Rowan, winter took a firm grip on the lakeland. A series of cold, windless days allowed ice to form between Hare Island and the mainland. Only to the west, where the lake was wider, was the ice having a harder time taking hold. The ice did interest them, and sometimes they'd climb to the top of the ridge between Wildwood and the lake and look out over the ice toward the north shore, a distant patchwork of green and white that they had never seen up close.

Whenever they went to the seedling grove or anywhere outside their clearing, the three snowshoe hares moved easily over the accumulating snow, and when the wind came whistling in from the north, the ridge along the lake and the surrounding trees sheltered the whole area. In their thick winter coats, Bramble and Kas were never uncomfortable, and even the elderly Rowan didn't seem to suffer.

Bramble and Kas were young hares out of their home element, easily influenced, and ready to do well or falter. Rowan was a strong and positive influence on both of them. He saw beyond Bramble's youthful insecurity, and in his quiet way, he planted seeds that helped Bramble grow more confident and look outward to his relationship with other hares. His effect on Kas was even more profound. Rowan was a dreamer and a thinker as well as a healer, and Kas began increasingly to see him as a role model. That set him on quite a different path from Bramble.

For some on Hare Island, it would have been better if this quiet interval had lasted until spring, but that was not to be.

Chapter 15
THE RACE

A race is a small journey.
It must begin.
It must end.
—Kas

One afternoon when Bramble arrived from a long excursion on the lakeshore, Kas hailed him and said, "Guess what? Rowan is getting ready for a Moon Ceremony. All the hares will be there, and we're invited."

"What's it all about?"

"Rowan will perform some kind of ritual, and he'll bless the medicines he's been making, including the one for us."

Three days later, under a clear sky, Rowan led Bramble and Kas toward the meeting place. It was crisp but not extremely cold. "It'll be perfect for the planned activities," Rowan said. "I'll be busy with the ceremonies, but you two join in with the others; we make this a day for all hares."

When they reached the clearing, Rowan took his leave. "Here we are," he told Bramble and Kas. "Enjoy yourselves."

Journey *to* Hare Island

The two friends, strangers to almost everyone, moved around and tried to look relaxed. Bramble saw a number of female hares spreading red-berried branches along the edge of the clearing. Tuagh and his companions, a rugged-looking bunch, stood in the centre, watching the females and joking with one another.

A paw touched Bramble's shoulder, and there was Rowan's friend Bayberry smiling at him. "How are you, Bramble? And Kas, Rowan speaks highly of you; he's glad you're taking an interest in healing."

Kas beamed.

Bayberry looked at each of them in turn and asked, "Are you going in the race?"

"Race?" said Bramble. "I didn't know there was one. I don't think so."

"Maybe you should, Bram," said Kas.

"I haven't raced against other hares in a long time."

"We'd be pleased to see you join in," said Bayberry. "It would give Tuagh some incentive because he's never been beaten. Come and I'll introduce you to the judges." He led Bramble and Kas over to three older hares. "Toker, Blaze, Powder, this is Kas, and this is Bramble. We've been urging Bramble to enter the race."

"I've heard of you two," said Blaze. "Bramble, is it? We'd love to have you. You needn't be shy about it: There'll be Tuagh and one or two others in front, a group in the middle, and then a few way back just out for fun. If you can stay with the middle group, you won't be embarrassed."

Kas urged Bramble, "Come on, Bram, one of us should enter, and I can't take four steps without falling."

Bramble looked over toward Tuagh, who was still talking to his friends. He was a strong-looking hare, and big. Bramble turned back to the judges and said, "Okay, then, tell me what to do."

"Good, good," said Blaze. "We've marked off a course just out from the shore. Come along when you see everyone moving down to the lake."

After the judges left, Bramble and Kas spent their time watching. Hares were moving in all directions—each, it seemed, with something to do. "At least they're not trying to stay a safe distance from us," Kas said.

On the south side of the clearing, hares started moving down toward the lake; Bramble and Kas followed. Spectators spread out along the beach to get a good view of the race. About twenty fit-looking hares gathered at the starting point, and Bramble joined them. Tuagh was on the far side of the group, which suited Bramble just fine.

Kas found himself a good viewing spot near the beach. A light wind was blowing from the south—not strong enough to influence the race in any way—and there was a clarity of light under a blue winter sky that would make viewing perfect for the spectators. Equally important, there were no signs of eagles or other predators that could have quickly put an end to the activities.

The First Hare raised his paw and spoke: "Friends, every year our younger hares test themselves to see who has the best speed and endurance; needless to say, these are important assets for hares. I'm proud to say that my son, Tuagh, won the race last year. I make no predictions for this year." There was laughter from most of the participants, and someone raised one of Tuagh's paws. He smiled.

The First Hare continued, "A feature of this year's race will be the entry of a visitor from the mainland, Bramble. Good luck, Bramble; you'll give incentive to our faster hares." There was a round of very polite thumping. Finally, the First Hare pointed down the ice to where a black branch could just be seen against the white snow. "We have a good course of packed snow. Participants, you must go round that far marker, return to the starting line here, and then race back to the far marker again and return. Are there any questions?"

One spectator shouted, "The prize! What's the prize?"

The First Hare looked over at the participants, as if on cue, and said, "As usual, when we have our ceremonies later, the winner will sit with this year's Queen, who happens to be Dawn." He smiled confidently. Again there was laughter, and some of Tuagh's cronies shouted his name.

This was Bramble's first glimpse of Dawn, who stood near the First Hare. She looked embarrassed, and perhaps not as happy as a Queen should be.

Bramble saw Kas wave at him from the crowd, and he nodded his head. Then, from a crouch, he watched the starter, who had raised his front paws. When he dropped his paws, they would be off, and with hare reflexes, all would get a fast start.

And so it was. When the race began, they all left quickly, and all held their own for a third of the way to the far marker. At that point a few hares, including Tuagh, began to pull ahead. Kas watched Bramble join a small group that settled in some distance behind the leaders. He looked relaxed, with his ears stretched along his back and his paws pounding the packed snow in an easy rhythm. The slowest group was already falling behind.

By the time the leading hares reached a point halfway to the first marker, it was hard for the spectators to tell what was happening, but there was still great excitement in the crowd. "Did you see Tuagh, already ahead?" shouted one.

"No coyote will ever catch him!" shouted another.

Cheers for one or two other hares could also be heard.

Only a blur could be seen as the first hares rounded the distant marker, and the noise died down as all eyes strained to pick out the front-runners, which was not easy with white coats against white snow. As they came closer, a sharp-eyed hare shouted, "It's Tuagh! I think he's increased his lead."

Soon Tuagh's group, flying across the snow, was clearly visible, and then the second group. Tuagh had doubled his lead, and the two hares closest to him were gradually being caught by Bramble's group.

Kas could see that many of the hares were struggling, but Tuagh still looked fresh, and when Bramble came abreast of the spectators, he showed no signs of tiring. As they made the turn and headed back for the distant marker, Kas hollered, "Good run, Bramble!" Someone in back of him laughed, but Bayberry, who had moved in beside Kas, said encouragingly, "Your friend is doing well."

Now the spectators were jumping up and down as the competitors made the distant turn the second time and headed for home. A group some way from Kas began to chant, "Tuagh, Tuagh, Tuagh!" Their shouts drowned out any cheers for others.

When the leaders reached the point halfway back to the finish line, the order of finish began to take shape: Tuagh was still in front by a big margin, and there were three hares in a second group. When Kas could make out individuals, he was overjoyed to see that Bramble was one of them; he could finish in the first three. The chant continued, "Tuagh, Tuagh, Tuagh!"

Then something happened that Kas would remember always. Bramble moved wide of the other two in his group. His stride lengthened. Kas had the impression that the two hares Bramble had been running with had given up. They hadn't, but Bramble had accelerated so much that he quickly left them behind. Spectators said after the race that it was hard for the eye to follow Bramble as he caught and passed Tuagh only five hare lengths from the finish line, and the judge standing beside the line swore that Bramble wasn't even breathing heavily when he won the race.

There were cheers from isolated points in the crowd, but for the most part, there was a hushed silence. Most hares were dumfounded by what they had seen, and not too happy to see a stranger win the race.

Kas, of course, was beside himself with excitement. He made his way quickly down to the finish line and pounded Bramble on the back. A few of the other participants came over and congratulated Bramble as well. Tuagh stood with three of his cronies, a scowl on his face as he stared at Bramble.

"If he wasn't an enemy before, he is now," Bramble said.

"There's no shame in losing if you've tried your best," Kas said.

"You really think he'll see it that way?" asked Bramble.

For a while after the race, the two friends explored east along the shore and found a quiet area with seedlings where they ate. In the late evening, they wandered back to the clearing so they could watch Rowan's ceremonies.

Chapter 16
THE WAY OF HARES

The moon hides behind the spruce boughs.
I see him peeking out.
And now and then, a night bird calls.
—Kas

As Bramble and Kas entered the clearing, Rowan called them over, his grizzled features lit with a smile. "They're all raving about your finish, Bramble," he said. "They think you may be the fastest hare they've ever seen. Come and I'll show you your places for the ceremony."

Kas had a choice viewing spot close to the front, and Bramble had a place of honour facing the First Hare. There was a cheer from the gathering as Dawn, Queen for the ceremony, was escorted in and seated on Bramble's right. They both stared straight ahead and waited for things to settle down. Rowan hadn't mentioned how attractive she was, and Bramble had trouble thinking of the right things to say. Finally he turned toward her and said quietly, "I'm happy to meet you, Dawn. I've already met your father through Rowan."

"I know who you are," said Dawn. "I was at the gathering when you first arrived, and my father said he talked to you at Rowan's. Congratulations on your race."

"Thank you. I know you were expecting to sit with someone else today; I hope I haven't spoiled your plans."

Dawn turned and pretended to study him from top to bottom, then she fixed him with a shy but pretty smile and said, "You'll do." They both started laughing, and for a few minutes they couldn't stop. Bramble had the odd feeling that life had taken a new turn.

The First Hare and a group of seniors were seated at the front, and several looked over when they heard the laughter. Dawn put a paw to her mouth and was suddenly quiet. Above them the moon appeared, freeing itself from the tops of the spruce trees to the south and setting its path directly over the clearing.

A hush settled in as the First Hare began to speak: "Fellow hares, today we celebrate our kinship with the spirits of our world and, of course, with the moon. Earlier we watched the annual race, this year won by a visitor, Bramble." There was some polite thumping, and Dawn looked at him again and smiled. "Last year's winner, Tuagh, did very well, but we all acknowledge Bramble's dramatic finish."

There was no resentment in the First Hare's voice, but when Bramble looked over, he could see that Tuagh's head was down. Dawn saw where he was looking and whispered, "Don't look at him, Bramble; he won't take this well, and he's dangerous when he's angry."

Bramble ventured, "Do you mean angry about the race?"

"About the race, about where you're seated. He's very jealous."

"So you two are a pair?" Bramble asked.

"Because he's Tuagh, and his father is First Hare, he thinks he can have what he wants. No other hare dares look at me."

Bramble sat awkwardly in his seat, but a glimmer showed in his eyes. The First Hare said, "I now call upon Rowan to conduct the ceremonies."

Rowan entered through a gap in the bushes. Someone had placed a garland of winterberries around his neck, and the red berries stood out nicely against his white fur. He stood directly in front of the seniors, where he could be seen by all, and raised his front paws toward the heavens. There was silence as he began, "Listen, and heed our most sacred prayer, *The Way of Hares:*

"This is the way of hares, and has been since the world began. We are hares, strong of limb and heart, and swift as the wind. We are born with eyes wide open, for we live perilous lives. Yet we survive in forest, and on mountain and plain, on desert, tundra, and grassland. To some, we symbolize the relentless energy of life. To others we are tricksters and witches, mad under the spring moon.

"Here in the northern forests, our coats white in winter and dark in summer, we offer this prayer to the moon: Keep us always free under the spruce boughs and in the alder groves, protect us from our enemies, keep the great sickness away from our forms, let our leverets chase each other forever on the edges of the clearings, give us moonlight to guide us through the snows of winter and the flowery meadows of summer, until we return at last to the Great Spirit."

Dawn turned toward Bramble and whispered, "Now he'll explain how the Moon Hare began."

Rowan continued in a more relaxed tone:

"There once was a hare, a fox, and a deer who lived peacefully together. One day an old man came into their territory who was actually the Great Spirit himself. The Great Spirit wanted to test the animals to see if they were generous enough to their fellow creatures, so he asked them to find him something to eat. They went off willingly.

— 80 —

Journey to Hare Island

Soon the fox brought back some apples that had fallen from a tree. Then the deer came with some grain from a nearby field. The old man made a fire and made bread from the grain. Then he roasted the apples and sat down to eat. After a time the hare came hopping back, looking quite sad. "I couldn't find any food, sir," he said, "but you can throw me into the fire for your main course." The hare was about to jump into the fire himself when the old man held him back. "My good friend, you are clearly the most generous of my creatures. I'm so impressed that I'm going to keep you by my side." So by magic, he threw the hare all the way up to the moon, there to stay and prepare elixirs for the Great Spirit. And it is said, by the healers and sages amongst the hares, that his image can still be seen if you look up very carefully when the moon is full."

Rowan left the clearing.

Bramble looked around at the gathered hares. Moonlight sparkled from their coats and from the snow that covered the ground and the branches of the spruce trees. It was a setting for magic, of whatever kind. He looked back as Rowan came into the clearing again, this time accompanied by two assistants carrying pouches. They placed the pouches in front of Rowan and moved off to the side. The healer looked up at the moon and once more extended his front paws:

"Immortal Moon Hare, companion to the gods, we ask you to bless our gathering and the elixirs we place before you."

He moved his paws over the elixirs and then paused, and Bramble saw that all present were looking skyward. When he himself looked up at the full moon, he saw, clearly outlined, the shape of the Moon Hare, as it always had been. He looked over at Dawn and saw her eyes were shining. Rowan spoke again:

"In return for your protection, oh Moon Hare, we vow to live in accordance with our ancient customs and traditions."

— 81 —

He lowered his paws and said to the gathering, "And now, my friends, be faithful to these promises. Return to your forms with the knowledge that the Moon Hare has blessed our gathering and has given me the means to do my healer's work if sickness comes to any of us."

There was a stir as the gathering broke up. Dawn touched Bramble's shoulder and said, "Remember, stay clear of Tuagh if you can." She looked over anxiously to where Tuagh sat.

"I'm not afraid of Tuagh," Bramble said.

Dawn got up as if to go but turned back, hesitated a moment, and then said, "I hope we can be friends." Then her face clouded over. "I have to go; I think Tuagh is coming this way." She left and joined other does who were leaving the clearing.

Kas approached Bramble. "Let's head for home," said Kas, "or should we find Rowan and ask if he needs help with anything?"

They were looking for Rowan when Bramble felt a push on his back. When he turned, Tuagh was standing very close. He spoke directly into Bramble's face: "You think you're pretty good, but let me give you some advice: Stay away from Dawn; she's not for the likes of you. You and that other trespasser keep to yourselves until we can send you back to the mainland."

Fur rose all the way down Bramble's back, but he fought hard not to let his anger show. His first priority was his duty to Alder Grove, so he didn't answer Tuagh the way he wanted to. "Thanks for your advice," he said. He turned away and started for Wildwood, Kas following along.

"Who does he think he is?" said Kas.

"We're strangers here," said Bramble. Then he stopped and touched the scar on his cheek. He looked back toward the clearing. "But there's got to be something we can do for Dawn."

They were halfway home when Rowan called from behind, "Hello there, could you youngsters give me some help?" The old hare's neck was bending from the weight of four large pouches, which Bramble and Kas took from him.

"Sorry, Rowan," said Bramble, "we looked for you after the ceremony, but then we got distracted."

"Yes, I saw Tuagh talking to you. So he wasn't praising you for your win? Some of his friends are saying you shouldn't have been allowed in the race; they think that foolishness lessens your victory. But you *will* have to be careful when you're away from Wildwood."

They went on in cheerless silence for a time, and then a smile broke through on Rowan's face. "By the way," he said, "I was happy to see you make friends with Dawn."

Chapter 17

DANGEROUS VISITORS

It was morning and the Wildwooders were at breakfast, crushing buds and the tips of seedling branches with their teeth and imagining the scent of flowers and the hum of summer insects. Spring would soon be here.

Suddenly Bramble's ears twitched. "I hear something on the path," he said, "moving fast." They crouched, ready to bolt, but then heard a hare calling, "Rowan, Rowan! Where are you?"

"Over here!" shouted Rowan, and a young hare appeared, fighting for breath. "A group of animals were spotted leaving the mainland," the young hare said. "We're sure it's coyotes. Hide, Rowan, but don't leave tracks into your hiding place." It was obvious he was reciting something he had been told to say. "I have to go." He turned quickly, took several deep breaths, and rushed back the way he had come.

Rowan waved to Bramble and Kas to follow and started down the path. "They remind me I'm old and slow; I'll have to hide," said Rowan. "You two come toward the centre of the Island so you can go in any direction if you see a coyote. You can easily outrun them; just don't get yourself cornered. A few poor souls will get caught before they realize there's danger near."

Journey *to* Hare Island

Bramble put his front paws out and stopped the other two. "Rowan, will word get to Bayberry's?"

"A good question; we won't know until the coyotes leave."

"That might be too late," said Bramble, "I'm going east." He sprinted away before the others had time to object.

Bramble felt his heart pounding as he flew along the trail. He turned at the fork and thundered down the long eastern stretch, his feet throwing up white puffs every time he hit snow. He wasn't sure exactly how far Waterside was, but suddenly he came upon Bayberry on the trail, dashing back and forth like a leveret.

Bramble shouted at the old hare, "Bayberry, where is she?"

"The east end. She doesn't know. What can I do?"

Bramble said firmly, "Okay, go find a hiding place, and I'll look after Dawn. Get going, Bayberry; she'll be angry if you stay here."

Bayberry watched Bramble speed away and then rushed the other way down the trail, calling Dawn's name as he went.

Bramble could see Dawn's tracks wherever a patch of snow covered the trail. The coyotes would spot them as well. He noticed that there were no trees out here on the point, only several clumps of bushes, so hiding would be difficult. At last, way up the southern shore, he saw Dawn.

When Bramble got closer, Dawn came up from the shore, a surprised look on her face. "Bramble, I didn't expect to see you today."

"Dawn, we're in danger. Coyotes were sighted and are no doubt on the Island now. The older hares, including your

— 85 —

father, are hiding. It's too late to go west, but we could get cornered out here."

Dawn lifted a front paw toward Bramble and asked, "You came down here to warn me? What about you?"

"Never mind that; tell me what the coyotes do when they reach the Island?"

"They make a sweep to catch hares by surprise; they hope they haven't been spotted coming to the Island. They don't take time to search out all the hiding places; they leave quickly in case the ice shifts." The tone of her voice changed, and she whispered, "They got my mother."

"But they won't get us. Will they come this far down?"

"I'm sure they will; they'll see our tracks."

"Let's go to the point and take a look," said Bramble. They went to the very end of the Island and looked over the lake. They'd be seen and tracked down if they tried to escape across the ice. He turned toward Dawn and said, "Okay, we have to do some running around. You take one side of the trail, I'll take the other. Make tracks into every clump of bushes. Cross your own path as often as you can. And hurry."

"But Bramble, we'll still be here."

"I have another idea. Just do this first."

They both raced around frantically until there were trails to every clump of bushes, then Bramble called to Dawn and they returned to the very tip of the Island. He pointed to several blocks of ice that had piled up near the shore and asked, "See that first block? Can you jump that far? It's flat on top so you'll land okay. I'll go first to make sure it can be done."

Dawn grimaced, but she nodded agreement. Bramble turned toward the ice, crouched down, and jumped, drawing his legs up and using them to cushion his landing. He looked back at Dawn and braced himself as she followed his lead. She landed a bit short but, with his help, scrambled to the top.

As they balanced themselves, Bramble looked farther out. He saw a ridge of snow big enough to hide behind. "Follow me," he said. One after the other, they jumped and landed just beyond the ridge. Immediately they both crouched down. "There are no tracks," Bramble whispered. "The wind's from the west so they won't scent us. We've got a good chance." He didn't have to tell Dawn to stay quiet and still; that was instinctive for all hares when danger was close.

Bramble could feel Dawn shivering by his side. They heard only the wind for some time. Then they were startled by a coyote yipping close by, and soon coyotes were signalling to one another from all over the point; every clump of bushes was being searched. They waited, hardly breathing, and gradually the coyote voices receded. Then, just when they thought they were safe, something scratched at the ice between them and the shore. Their leg muscles tightened; they would spring instantly away if a coyote appeared. But nothing happened. Very slowly, Bramble raised his head and looked toward the shore: A herring gull was perched not far away, scratching at the ice to free some morsel of food. Relief flooded through Bramble's body. He touched Dawn with a comforting paw, and they went back to the shore and looked around. The coyotes had left plenty of evidence that they had been there: Tracks followed every lead that Bramble and Dawn had created, and snow had been dislodged from every clump of bushes. But they couldn't hear even distant coyote voices.

"You said they'd leave the Island once they'd scoured it?" asked Bramble.

"That's what I've always heard."

They started down the main trail, stopping to listen frequently. Before reaching the fork that led off to Wildwood, they saw a horrible sight: blood stains against the white snow and clumps of fur. Dawn whimpered but was afraid to look closer. Bramble nuzzled her shoulder; he knew what she was thinking.

They turned a corner and saw a large group of hares gathered on the path. Dawn held her breath, then recognized Bayberry and rushed to his side. "You're safe!"

Bayberry went back and forth between Dawn and Bramble several times, grinning and nuzzling them. Finally he could speak: "I was afraid for both of you. The coyotes are gone, but we're not sure how many hares were killed. Did you manage to hide?"

"Bramble figured out how to fool them," Dawn said. "He saved my life."

Bramble tilted his head down as they were surrounded by hares who insisted on hearing their story. He let Dawn do the talking. A small group in back seemed less interested in his heroics; in the centre of the group was Tuagh.

Soon more hares came from the west, Kas and Rowan amongst them. After the greetings and the expressions of relief, they wanted to hear the story as well. Afterwards, Bayberry and Dawn decided to leave. "We're going," Bayberry said, "but you and Kas come visit us, Bramble, and thank you again." Dawn gave Bramble a final look of gratitude, glanced nervously over at Tuagh, and followed her father down the path.

The First Hare's paw was on Bramble's shoulder. "You and Kas are most welcome to stay on the Island as long as you'd like, but now I must take my old bones back to my form."

Kas and Rowan had started for home, so Bramble took his leave and followed. Before he left the main trail, two hares

Journey to Hare Island

came up beside him—friends of Tuagh, he guessed. "Sorry, am I in your way?" Bramble asked.

The larger of the two said, "Weren't you told to stay away from Dawn?"

"Let the coyotes have her, you mean? Haven't you had enough excitement for one day?"

"Never mind today; we're talking about the future. Never again, in other words." He raised his front paw to make his point on Bramble's shoulder, but Bramble got a back paw far enough over to trip the surprised hare, who sprawled awkwardly onto the path. He got up quickly and both hares turned to attack, but when Bramble held his ground, they stopped.

"So tell me," said Bramble, "why should I listen to you where Dawn is concerned?"

There was an awkward silence. Bramble looked around, but Tuagh was nowhere in sight. "I'll be on my way then."

They moved aside, but as Bramble passed, one of them said lamely, "Just remember."

Bramble laughed and kept going.

At Wildwood, Rowan and Kas were waiting on the path. "We were starting to worry about you," said Rowan.

Bramble shrugged and said, "I had a brief conversation with a couple of Tuagh's crowd; they weren't thanking me for protecting Dawn."

"I thought there'd be follow-up to today's events," Rowan said. "Was Tuagh there?"

"I didn't see him, and I looked around."

"He won't go against his father openly, but sadly, he's not to be trusted. Let's go in and get some rest."

Chapter 18
CHANGE OF COMMAND

One afternoon when Bramble came out from his form, he saw small pools of water on the surface of the path. He felt the sun on his fur and remembered warm afternoons at Alder Grove romping with his friends. What was going on at the Grove now, and when would the ice on the lake break up so he could go home?

His daydream was interrupted when a senior hare came up the path, greeted him, and went in to find Rowan. After a short time, he reappeared and went back down the trail. When Rowan and Kas emerged, the older hare had a troubled look on his face. "I've been called to a meeting with senior hares, and they want me to visit the First Hare; he isn't well. I'll be a while." He plodded slowly down the path, a pouch of medicine around his neck.

"Rowan is old himself," said Kas. "He'll be badly missed when he dies. I'm learning an awful lot from him, Bram. What would you say if I decided to stay here for a time and go back to Alder Grove later?"

Bramble sat quietly for a few moments, looking at Kas, then said, "I always thought we'd go back together, but if you think staying would be best, you'll have my support." Bramble was trying hard to sound mature, but his voice revealed the leveret that was still in his heart. "If you stay, it won't be for too long, will it?"

Kas was moved by Bramble's response. "Thanks, Bram. You'll always be my best friend." He turned away and pretended to chew on a birch twig.

When Rowan came back toward evening, he had a grave look on his face, "I have news. The First Hare is weak; I fear he'll die soon. Then there could be problems. The seniors have asked me to be First Hare, but I'm much more useful to everyone doing what I do out here; I wouldn't be happy, or successful, as First Hare. They'll offer the position to Ragweed, and he'll accept. He's well intentioned but easily influenced, and Tuagh will have his ear. It's hard to say what Tuagh will do."

Bramble asked, "Tuagh won't hurt you, Rowan?"

"No, they need their healer, and I'm not a threat to Tuagh. I'll be left alone. So will Bayberry. I can protect Kas by claiming him as an assistant, but Tuagh is seething with anger at you, Bramble. He should be thanking you for saving Dawn, but that wouldn't be Tuagh. In short, you'll have to leave the Island soon. The problem is that right now, the timing is bad: It's dangerous to cross the ice while it's breaking up, and you can't go by water until the ice is gone. And remember, Tuagh knows every inch of the Island, so it would be useless to hide."

A few days later, Bramble sat on the shore near Wildwood and inspected the ice. Cracks were visible, but complete breakup would be a slow process. He'd have to leave from the south side of the Island, but he guessed the ice situation would be similar over there.

One morning, before the first signs of dawn, an excited voice called from outside on the path: "Rowan, the First Hare is asking for you; he can't get up from his form."

"Come in," said Rowan. A young hare entered, and Rowan asked, "Has he been eating?"

"Not a thing for two or three days."

"Right. Go tell them I'm on my way."

Rowan turned to Bramble and Kas. "Kas, get me the pouch with the mix of medicines, and take the large pouch yourself, if you don't mind." Kas hurried to find the two pouches. "The signs are not good," Rowan said. "The First Hare is dying. Bramble, you know where the elixir for Alder Grove is?"

"The pouch on the far right in the central alcove."

"You'd better leave it here until we know for sure." Rowan hollered in to Kas, "We have to go!" He turned to Bramble again and said, "If you came with us to the fork, you could go to Waterside and see Dawn and Bayberry." Bramble nodded, and Rowan continued, "I'll send Kas with news of the First Hare's condition. Tuagh will probably act against you as soon as his father dies, and he'll try to claim Dawn, a prospect that disturbs all of us. You'll have some decisions to make, Bramble."

Bramble, Kas, and Rowan huddled together briefly at the fork to say their goodbyes. Then, not slowed by the older hare,

Journey to Hare Island

Bramble hurried toward Waterside. Twice on his way, he heard a hare coming toward him and jumped into the bushes; it would be safer if no one else knew where he was heading. He was breathing heavily when he reached Waterside; he stopped for a moment to catch his breath and gather his thoughts, then he called out, "Bayberry, Dawn, are you home?"

"Come in, please."

Bayberry saw the look on Bramble's face and immediately asked, "Is something wrong?"

"Rowan's been called to the First Hare's form. They think he's dying."

"Oh, dear," said Bayberry. "We knew this was coming, but I thought he'd last until spring."

"He's been fair to Kas and me," said Bramble, "and he's made Tuagh more cautious. Rowan says when the First Hare dies, Tuagh will deal with me right away. I have no choice but to leave the Island."

There was a gasp from Dawn, and Bayberry looked dismayed. "Oh my, Bramble," he said, "this is terrible news; the ice is just starting to break up. What'll you do?"

"I'll have to go over the ice, and the longer I wait, the more dangerous that will be."

"But there may be open water," said Bayberry.

"None of my options are good. If I do nothing, I'll soon be a captive, or more likely dead. If I try to hide, Tuagh will find me. Besides, I have to get the elixir home to Alder Grove; I can't give up on that."

Bramble was silent as his words took their effect on father and daughter. Gradually the look on Bayberry's face turned to resolve, and he said, "You two go out front and see what the ice is doing. I want to think."

Dawn led Bramble out to a cliff overlooking the lake. The ice sheet looked continuous from the Island to the shore, but with snow and ice ridges here and there, it was impossible to tell how chancy a crossing might be. "Oh, Bramble," said Dawn, "I don't know what to say. You're in danger because of me, and I might not see you again."

Bramble looked out at the ice, then back at his friend. "Except for the dangers you'd face, Dawn, I'd ask you to go with me." Bramble looked down and then out at the ice again, surprised by his own boldness.

Dawn was quiet for only a moment, then she moved closer to Bramble." I couldn't leave my father alone or I wouldn't hesitate; I'd be happy to share your dangers."

Neither had heard Bayberry approaching, but he was standing just behind them. They were startled when he spoke. "Nonsense, Dawn. Did I raise you to be with an oaf like Tuagh when you could be with Bramble? Which option do you think would make me happy in my old age? You must go!"

Dawn turned in surprise and looked at Bayberry. "But what would happen to you?"

"More nonsense. I have more friends than Tuagh has. When your mother died, I vowed to look after you until you could make your own way. I think that time has come." He turned to Bramble and said, "If you must cross the ice, I have a suggestion." He pointed out over the lake. "The ice breaks up first out on the main lake; it takes longer here on the bay. If you leave from this end of the Island and bear east toward the inner bay as you cross, you'll end up a little farther from Alder Grove, but the crossing should be safer."

As Bayberry was finishing, they heard someone calling from out front. "That's Kas," said Bramble.

Kas came quickly out to where they stood. "Rowan says the First Hare will die within the hour. He wants you to get the packet and leave, Bram."

Bramble had a grim look on his face. "Kas, I'm going across the ice." He looked over at Dawn, and she nodded her head. "Dawn is coming with me. Are you sure you won't come?"

"I'm not ready yet, Bram, but I'll be thinking of the two of you. Now please go get the elixir; I'll stay with Dawn and Bayberry until you're back."

Chapter 19
THE CROSSING

A turn in the path,
A shift in the wind,
Sometimes the parting is forever.
—Kas

Bramble left Waterside quickly. He saw no one on his way to Wildwood, found the pouch, looped it around his neck with its root handle, and left for what he guessed would be the last time.

If he wasn't seen on his way back to Waterside, he and Dawn could cross the ice slowly, going around open water. If he met someone and word got back to Tuagh, they would have to sprint for the mainland, and that would be dangerous.

He passed the fork and started through the more settled area. Suddenly, as he turned a corner, a female hare stood directly in his way. Bramble managed to stay calm. He stepped around her, offered her a greeting, and moved on. He hoped she would have no reason to mention their meeting to anyone.

He was past the settled area when he felt that someone was watching him. Was he imagining things? Then a movement in nearby bushes caught his attention, and in the lengthening shadows, he saw a hare standing still and looking in his direction. When he moved to get a better look, the shadows shifted and the hare was gone. All he could do was keep going.

Kas and the others looked anxiously toward him when he arrived at Waterside. Bramble reported, "Rowan wasn't at Wildwood; he must still be with the First Hare. On the way back, I saw two hares and they saw me; word could get to Tuagh, so we'll have to leave right away."

Kas brought some green twigs over to Bramble and said, "Dawn has already had some." Bramble could eat only a small amount. He looked up at his friend and replied, "Thanks, Kas. When we leave, go through the woods to get to Wildwood. Promise me; if Tuagh finds out you were here, he'll punish you."

Kas stood next to Bramble, while Dawn leaned her head on Bayberry's shoulder. She whispered, "You'll always be in my heart, Father."

Bayberry had trouble speaking but managed to whisper, "Good luck. Now go, and you as well, Kas; tell Rowan I'll visit when things settle down." All four went to the front trail. Kas exchanged one last look with Bramble, then started for home. He angled north to enter the woods. They could barely see him turn and wave in the gathering darkness; then he was gone.

Bramble lowered his head to Bayberry in respect and said, "I'll look after her." Then he and Dawn headed east. When they looked back, they saw Bayberry watching. "He'll be fine, Dawn," said Bramble. "His friends will protect him." They turned and hurried up the trail.

Dusk gave way to night, and a nearly full moon shone from a cloudless sky. "The moonlight will be great for seeing open water," Bramble told Dawn, "but it'll make us easier to spot."

They reached the tip of the Island and looked out over the ice. Bramble pointed to the brightest light showing on the mainland and said, "We'll aim for that." Dawn looked back up the trail and sighed, "My home." Bramble nuzzled her briefly on the cheek, then they climbed down to the shore. Now a mostly level expanse stretched out before them. Dawn moved to Bramble's shoulder, and they started across.

After a time, Bramble stopped and looked at Dawn. "How do you feel?"

"I feel sad, and afraid, but glad to be here with you. I'm not tired, if that's what you mean."

The light on the mainland seemed brighter, but Hare Island still looked close. When Bramble looked back at their departure point, he gasped. Four hares were moving along the edge of the cliff, clearly visible in the moonlight.

"What did you see?" asked Dawn.

"We're being followed. Now we have to sprint." The wind was brisk and coming from the south, so any open water would be near the mainland shore. They would not be caught at this speed, but Tuagh, at least, would not be falling behind. The mainland loomed closer; if they could get there first, they'd be able to hide in the woods along the lake.

Suddenly they came to a ribbon of water running parallel to the shore. Bramble looked frantically right and then left. "Dawn, follow me; your father said keep to the east." They sped along the edge of the ice and saw the gap narrowing slightly, but when they looked back, they realized that making the turn had reduced their lead. Bramble pointed and asked Dawn, "Can you jump across?"

Dawn looked back in panic at the pursuers, who were approaching quickly. "I'll try."

"We'll take a run at it," said Bramble. They moved back from the water. Dawn accelerated and was a blur in the moonlight as she jumped. She landed safely on the other side, but the wind had picked up and was slowly widening the gap. Bramble exploded toward the water and jumped. He landed on the very edge of the shore ice and slid to safety. Across from them, four hares now stood looking at the open water.

Bramble saw Tuagh's three companions arguing with him and guessed they were trying to get him to face reality: They might get across the gap, but what if the breakup came? It could be a month before they were able to return to Hare Island. Tuagh left them and moved back and forth along the edge of the ice. Then it seemed his desire for revenge won out. He moved back, sprinted to the edge, and jumped. He was at least as strong as Bramble, and almost as fast, but he was heavier, and the wind had now widened the gap. He almost made it, but his weight pulled him down a fraction too soon. With a sickening thud, he hit the side of the ice and fell, apparently lifeless, into the freezing water.

"We can't wait to see what those others will do," said Bramble. "Let's get out of here." He and Dawn turned and fled into the dense forest that fringed the lake.

Chapter 20
HOMEWARD BOUND

Dawn glanced under every branch and kept testing the air for danger; the mainland woods were foreign to her, so Bramble stayed close. He asked her often if she wanted to rest, but she preferred to put distance between them and anyone who might be following. They went inland and then turned west when they came to a large trail. The forest was dense and dark, with only occasional streaks of moonlight reaching the forest floor, and they served only to exaggerate the darkness.

With the first glimmer of morning, they found a sheltered spot under a fir tree and settled down close to each other. "We'll eat before we start moving again," said Bramble. Dawn was hungry, but otherwise she seemed content. She moved even closer to Bramble and drifted off to sleep.

Bramble awoke with Dawn nudging him on the shoulder. "Bramble, did you hear that?"

He listened and asked, "What? I can't hear anything."

"There's no wind now, but I'm sure I heard branches moving."

Journey *to* Hare Island

"It's time to get going anyway; I'll take a look." Bramble was able to follow their tracks for a short distance behind the fir tree. Then he stopped: Visible in the snow were the paw prints of a hare who must have been following them. The hare had moved around and then crouched in the snow within sight of their tree. Then it had gotten up and followed its own tracks back along the trail. Bramble hesitated a moment, then called to Dawn, "Take a look at this!" He pointed out the third set of tracks and stood by as she read the story clearly visible in the snow.

"We're being followed. It's Tuagh or one of his gang, isn't it?"

She could be right, but there were other possibilities. "We'll have to be careful," said Bramble, "but this could simply be a local checking us out. Someone like Tuagh would have attacked us while we were asleep."

"Perhaps," Dawn replied. She didn't sound convinced.

By the middle of the afternoon, the trees were thinning out, and finally they came to a flat expanse where snow held on in patches. It was Big Swamp. High over the swamp, but closer to the shore of the lake, an eagle soared. They couldn't enter such an exposed area with an eagle around. "We'll cross in the morning," Bramble said.

At first light Bramble led the way into Big Swamp, looking back often to make sure Dawn was with him. There were countless ponds to skirt and small streams to get across, but there was no sign of an eagle. They passed the bush where he and Kas had sheltered, and he told Dawn about falling through the ice and the strange deer. Early in the afternoon, they jumped over a final stream and reached the western boundary.

Big Swamp had been hard on their bodies and their nerves, so they pushed in under low-hanging spruce boughs for the night.

This time it was Bramble who awoke first. He shook Dawn and whispered, "Something's moving out there. You go out the back way and hide; if this is Tuagh or one of his pals, I'm not going to run." Bramble's body was tense, and stress contracted the muscles around his face. There was a painful note in his voice when he said, "If I'm not around to guide you, continue along the lake and you'll find Alder Grove. Talk to the First Hare and tell him your story. If he's not there, talk to my littermate Thorny or to a hare called Shiver. Now go. If this is something big and I have to run, I'll meet you here later."

Dawn crept away on legs rubbery with fear, while Bramble steeled himself for an attack. He heard something coming directly toward him; his nose confirmed that the intruder was a snowshoe hare. Then, from a short hop away, a voice called, "Is that you in there, Bramble? It's Dusty; I was hopin' I'd see you on your way back."

Bramble took a deep breath and sank down on his hind legs. "Dusty, you almost scared my tail off."

There was a rustling of branches and Dusty entered, his right ear hanging awkwardly down the side of his head. "Wait here, Dusty," said Bramble. "I have to get someone."

After a short time, Bramble returned with Dawn, and Dusty looked surprised. "*Crow feathers,* I expected Kas."

Bramble put a paw on Dawn's shoulder. "Dusty, meet Dawn. She's from Hare Island, but she's coming to Alder Grove with me." Dawn was so relieved that she couldn't say anything.

"Pleasure, Dawn," said Dusty. He made a polite bow. "But is Kas okay?"

"He's fine. He's studying to be a healer with a friend on Hare Island."

"A healer?" said Dusty, "He didn't mention that."

"It's a long story."

"So your trip was successful?" He looked bashfully at Dawn. "Aside from makin' a friend, I mean?"

Bramble pointed to the pouch lying on the ground. "We do have something we're taking back to Alder Grove."

"Good for you, youngster. I didn't think you'd reach Hare Island, but I've been watching for you anyway. It's been a long winter, but sickness didn't show up here. Anyway, I'll make up for scarin' you with a good breakfast; you fill me in on your trip, and then we can all skedaddle."

Dusty had exaggerated: Breakfast was a sparse meal of birch buds and twigs. As they ate, Bramble told Dusty all he could think of about his adventures. Not long after that, Dawn and Bramble were again travelling west, Dawn working out the rubbery feeling she still felt in her legs.

Chapter 21

DEAD END

The sunset
Bleeds into the lake,
Drop by drop.
—Kas

Several mornings later, Bramble and Dawn were skirting the north side of a large pond. To their right lay a gravel beach, and beyond that was the vast expanse of ice and water that was the mother lake itself. Dawn, who had lived only with the smaller size of the bay, was amazed at the new scale of things.

By noon, the shore had risen steeply into a cliff. Bramble was keen to spot signs of home, so they climbed the snow-covered headland and looked out. To the east they could see, way off in the distance, the tip of Hare Island; directly in front of them was the lake at its widest point, but to the west, their cliff climbed higher still and blocked the view. Bramble decided to climb to the highest point, but it was a difficult climb, so he suggested that Dawn wait below.

"I'm already a bit dizzy looking out there," Dawn said, "and that climb does seem rugged, but I'm nervous staying alone."

"You'll see me all the time, and I'll be right back."

Journey *to* Hare Island

Bramble gave the pouch to Dawn for safekeeping, then hopped from rock to rock, scrambled up sections of loose gravel, and was soon high above the place where Dawn sat waiting. He waved, then moved carefully to the outer edge, which was a dangerous height above the water. The face of the cliff below him fell to Dawn's level, and then farther still to the rocks below. When he looked west, he saw three headlands, blue in the afternoon haze, with suggestions of white showing here and there. Alder Grove was surely just in from one of them.

He was taking a last look when he heard a scream. He rushed to the inner edge; Dawn was on the ground, struggling against a large hare. Even from this height, he could make out who it was: Tuagh had survived his encounter with the ice wall and had waited to catch one of them alone. Now he was trying to tear at Dawn's stomach with his powerful hind legs.

Bramble charged recklessly down the incline, shouting Tuagh's name. When Bramble drew close, Tuagh pushed away from Dawn and braced himself for the charge. Bramble hit Tuagh head on. Both were knocked to the ground but were back on their feet quickly. Bramble stood on his hind legs, ready to scratch and fend off with his front paws and to kick with his hind paws when he saw an opening, but with his greater bulk, Tuagh knocked him over backwards. Tuagh tried to get close, but Bramble spun away and stood with his back to a large boulder near the edge of the cliff. When he glanced at the rocks below, he knew what Tuagh would try to do.

There was an ugly wound on one side of Tuagh's face, and his fur was a patchwork of white and brown, still with streaks of red where blood had dripped from his wound. Despite his appearance, he had lost none of his strength or speed. When

Tuagh's charge came, Bramble made a last-moment shift sideways, but Tuagh had anticipated his move and caught enough of Bramble's shoulder to knock him backwards again. This time Bramble's head hit solid rock. He tried to rise, but his legs wouldn't cooperate. Worse still, he had rolled sideways along the face of the boulder and was lying at the very edge of the cliff.

As Tuagh started his final rush, Dawn uttered a piercing scream, and Tuagh turned his head briefly. Bramble was desperate, but he managed to get one hind foot against the ground before the big hare reached him. He caught Tuagh in the chest with his other hind foot and heaved upward. Tuagh twisted his body in the air in a desperate attempt to regain his footing, but before he could, his momentum carried him over the edge. Bramble and Dawn heard a tortured cry as Tuagh hit the rocks below.

Dawn went quickly to Bramble's side. "Are you okay?"

One shoulder was sore, and his head was still woozy, but he hadn't suffered any serious damage. He got slowly to his feet, leaned against Dawn, and asked, "How about you?"

"More frightened than hurt. I was watching you up there when he came from behind. After that it's all a blur." She looked toward the cliff. "Do you think he survived the fall?"

They went to the edge and looked down. Tuagh had landed on a large boulder at the foot of the cliff. His body was twisted awkwardly, and his head lay in a pool of blood. He would never bother anyone again.

"Oh," Dawn said, "how horrible!"

"At least we'll be safe now," said Bramble, "and so will your father, Kas, and Rowan; Tuagh's followers won't cause trouble without him."

Journey *to* Hare Island

They travelled more that day, but slowly; Bramble's limbs were sore from his headlong rush down the slope and from the battering Tuagh had given him. Even so, he took no comfort in the thought of Tuagh's body being carried away by a keen-sighted eagle, or being washed into the cold lake by the first waves that reached his resting place.

Chapter 22
THE ELIXIR

It's a long jump that makes no landing.
—Peter Rabbit

As the days passed, both Bramble and Dawn were eager to reach Alder Grove. Bramble wanted to bring the elixir home, and Dawn longed for a more settled life. They avoided speculating on how badly the winter had gone for Alder Grove, but Dawn knew it was a big worry for Bramble.

Late one evening, Bramble said with excitement, "We're only a few days from home. We have that grove of trees, a big expanse of alders, a valley with a stream, and then a final stand of spruce, and we'll be on the edge of our meadow." To Dawn, it sounded like a long way.

These weren't comfortable days. Spring was coming quickly to the lakeshore; instead of easy going along snow-covered trails, Bramble and Dawn now splashed through mud or soggy moss, and it rained every day. They plodded on but stopped now and then to shake water from their fur. They were quickly soaked again, and finding a dry place to rest became difficult.

When they started down into a valley late one afternoon, Bramble suggested that they stop until morning: "There's a stream that could be high with all this rain." They managed to find a spot with dry leaves under a fallen tree. Bramble was tired and damp, but he was still excited. "We could be home by this time tomorrow. We'll see the First Hare right away about the elixir, and about you joining the community."

"Do you think he'll accept me?"

"I'm sure he will. I know he'll like you, and I've done everything he asked, so that should help. "

It was still raining when they set out next morning. Long before they reached the stream, they could hear it raging. When they stood on the bank of what should have been a medium-sized stream, they saw a wide torrent—and no way to get across.

They sat for a while looking at the water tumbling past. "We have to try something," Bramble said. He looked up and down the stream, then said, "Let's explore upstream." They moved with care along the bank, staying well away from the edge.

Eventually, they came to a fallen tree perched halfway across the stream. They sat and studied it carefully for a time, then Bramble stood. "I think we can jump across from the outer end," he told Dawn. "You go first, but make it good, or you'll end up in the lake."

Dawn crept carefully through the branches to the end of the tree and crouched to get the maximum spring from her legs. She was ready to go when Bramble cried, "Look upstream!" A large log had rounded the nearest bend and was bearing down on them. "Hurry, it's going to bang into this tree!" yelled Bramble.

Dawn jumped but, in her panic, misjudged the distance. She landed with only her front legs gripping the bank and her hind legs showing white just under the water. She could barely hold on. Bramble moved in panic through the branches, intending to jump as well, but just before he reached the end, a sharp branch snagged the pouch from around his neck, leaving it dangling over the water.

He had only an instant to consider: Turn, grab the pouch, and dart back to shore, or jump to the opposite bank and pull Dawn from the current. He took one step forward and pushed hard with his hind legs, landing on the bank just above Dawn. He reached down, and with all the strength he could muster with his front legs, he dragged her from the water. When he looked up, his worst fears were being realized: The floating log swept the tree from its moorings, and the tree rolled once and followed the larger log down the stream, but the pouch was nowhere to be seen. He told Dawn to stay where she was and rushed in panic along the bank. He saw the log and the tree just as they were washed into the lake, but there was no sign of the pouch. He made his way slowly back to Dawn and sat down heavily beside her. "I've lost it, Dawn, after all my efforts with Kas and with you. What will the First Hare say when I tell him I got this close and lost it?"

Dawn was crestfallen, too. She realized that in saving her, Bramble had sacrificed his dream of bringing the elixir home. There was nothing helpful she could say, so she simply moved closer to Bramble and let her head lean against his shoulder.

Halfway through the afternoon, they still sat together near the stream. Ironically, now that the rain had destroyed

Bramble's dream, the clouds gave way to a clear sky. An early robin landed on a branch above their heads and called cheerfully, but the two hares crouching below were unmoved. Dawn tried her best to comfort Bramble by saying, "You weren't being careless; your First Hare will understand."

"Well, Alder Grove deserved more from me, but I can't turn my back on my home now. Let's see if there's anything useful we can do." They stood, stretched their legs, and started on the last night of the journey.

Chapter 23

HOME AT LAST

The journey home is always different:
There are memories waiting to happen,
Promises to keep.
—Kas

"The last trees before the meadow," Bramble told Dawn. "We'll be there at first light, just when the Alder Grove hares are feeding." They hurried on.

Now the trees were behind them, and first light was showing. Bramble took in the whole scene, from the lake to the stand of spruce trees in the south. He sat back on his haunches and looked at Dawn. "This is the meadow, and over there is Alder Grove," he said. "There's no wind or rain this morning, and I can see grass along the edge of the alders. But no one is out there feeding. Not one!"

What did it mean? Bramble looked ready to go back to the woods, but Dawn kept watching the far side of the meadow, desperate to find some ray of hope. They sat and waited for a long time. Finally a hare moved out from the alders and began to feed. "Bramble!" Dawn said with excitement. "I see a hare now."

Bramble was up immediately. "Let's find out who it is," he said. When they got halfway across the meadow, the hare stood alert, his ears forward and his head up testing the breeze. He looked ready to bolt. Bramble called, "It's me, Bramble!"

The hare hesitated, then said, "Bramble, that can't be you?"

Bramble recognized the voice. "Sure it is, Stormy, and this is my friend Dawn."

"I'm glad to see you, Bramble, and welcome to your friend."

Bramble looked up and down the edge of the alders. "But where are the others?"

Stormy sat and shook his head. "We had a bad winter, Bramble, just as the First Hare had predicted. The sickness killed some and weakened others. Coyotes and owls saw their chance. I lost friends, and two of my littermates. We're a lot fewer now, and as you can see, some are so frightened they hardly come out to eat."

"What about the First Hare?"

Stormy looked over his shoulder and moved closer to Bramble. "The winter was hard on him. I've gathered enough food to keep us alive, but he's barely holding on. It doesn't help that some call him weak and blame him for the winter. They've been talking of moving somewhere else."

"What?" said Bramble. "Leave Alder Grove? Whose idea was that?"

Stormy glanced over his shoulder again. "Sprucie is their leader; there were lots of desperate hares around, and he discovered he could influence them."

Bramble shook his head. "The First Hare is lucky to have you, Stormy. Tell him we're here and say we'll come when he wants us. We'll be at my old form."

Bramble led Dawn toward the lake and then into the alders. He stopped and looked around: Small branches littered the run, and spikes of wild rose and other plants grew out from both sides. "I'd hate to be running from a coyote along here," he said. Dawn followed him through a dense tangle of alders and rosebushes that opened to a clearing.

"This is it," said Bramble. "This is where Kas and I lived. Over there's a second way out, and a few hops beyond is a cliff overlooking the lake, just like at your father's." He looked around the clearing. "I have to clean in here, too."

"It's great," said Dawn. "I guess Kas isn't here to complain if I use his form?"

Bramble sat down and faced Dawn, a troubled look on his face. "I was afraid to ask Stormy about my friends. As for Sprucie, I've never trusted him. I can imagine how the First Hare must feel."

Bramble and Dawn had only bits of troubled sleep before Stormy asked to enter. "The First Hare wants to see both of you."

"Tell him we'll be there right away," said Bramble. He managed to stretch himself awake, but stress and weeks of physical exertion showed. He looked over at Dawn and asked, "Are you ready?"

"I guess so. Is there anything you want me to say or not say?"

"Be yourself; I'm sure he'll like you. He won't be happy about the elixir, though." As they went toward the centre of Alder Grove, they saw a few hares, but only at a distance, and always through a screen of bushes. Then they saw Stormy ahead, waiting to escort them in for their meeting.

The First Hare looked greyer around the muzzle and tired, but he brightened when he saw who was entering. "My dear Bramble, it's wonderful to see you. And who is your friend?"

Journey *to* Hare Island

Bramble led Dawn forward and said, "This is Dawn. She came with me from Hare Island. We hope she can stay in Alder Grove."

Dawn bowed her head in respect.

"Of course, Bramble," the First Hare said, "without any question if she's a friend of yours."

"Thank you," said Dawn. "I'll try to be worthy of your trust." She stepped back so the other two could talk.

The First Hare suddenly remembered and said, "And your friend Kas? I expected to see him as well."

"Kas is fine, and he was a big help on the journey." Bramble told the First Hare about Rowan, about Kas staying behind, and about his promise to return later to Alder Grove.

"Good for Kas, and we can certainly use a healer. Now tell me more about your travels."

Bramble touched the scar on his cheek lightly. "First Hare, I'll be happy to tell you all about the journey, but first I want to explain what happened yesterday." He described the rushing stream, the attempt to cross, and the loss of the elixir. When he finished, he sat back on his haunches. Dawn moved to his side.

The First Hare sat looking from one to the other. When he spoke, to Bramble's surprise, there was no anger in his voice. "Have you looked around Alder Grove and talked to your friends?"

"We've seen my old form, but we've spoken only to Stormy. He said there were deaths, and that some even talked about leaving Alder Grove. I find that hard to believe."

"Believe it, Bramble. In good time we'll discuss it, but only after you've seen a few other hares. Find your friends. Ask them about the winter. I want them to know you're back, and they should meet Dawn. Your arrival will please them. But before you go, do tell me about your journey and your time on Hare Island. In the evening when you come back, we'll discuss what to do about the situation here."

So Bramble talked about the journey and about his stay on Hare Island, until finally the First Hare declared himself satisfied. Then Bramble and Dawn left to make their visit around Alder Grove. Bramble still couldn't understand why the First Hare took the loss of the elixir so well, but he guessed the anger would show by the evening.

Chapter 24
ALDER GROVE

Even in Alder Grove,
When I hear a robin singing,
I long for Alder Grove.
—*Kas, with apologies to Basho*

Bramble and Dawn followed the edge of the meadow to the lake, and then went east into Alder Grove, passing their forms and continuing downhill toward the cove. Near the cove, water lay in puddles beside the path, and Dawn saw Bramble cringe and look away. "We call this Low End," he said. "It's wet and isn't great for forms or anything else. I spent my first weeks here, shivering most of the time. I'm lucky I survived." He stopped and forced himself to look in under the sparse alders. "My mother did the best she could, but she saw two of our litter die, and then she was killed herself. You'll meet Thorny; he's the only other one from my litter who survived."

Dawn could see the burden of Bramble's early experiences in his face, and having lost her own mother early, she understood. She touched Bramble's shoulder and said, "You and your littermate were amazing then, Bramble; most leverets would have died under those circumstances."

They went south along the edge of the cove. "Over here is a spot where we gathered as youngsters," said Bramble. "We had fun chasing each other and tumbling around." High bush cranberries surrounded the clearing ahead. On the shore of the cove, a hare sat by himself. A blue heron stood just offshore. The hare turned, looked, and then bounded to his feet, sending the heron off in search of a quieter spot. "Bramble, you're home. I knew you'd make it back."

Bramble and the other hare touched paws and sat facing each other. "Shiver, I'm glad to see you. Where's the rest of the crowd?"

"Did you just come back, Bramble?"

"I know you had a hard winter," said Bramble, "but our friends aren't all dead?"

"No, no," said Shiver. "Thorny is around, and Teaberry, but I'm sorry to tell you that Misty, and Flower, and Patches, are all dead."

Bramble reached out and touched Shiver's paw again. "Not little Misty? You two were always together." Then Bramble turned and said, "Dawn, this is my friend Shiver; we were close friends, and still are I hope?"

"Always, Bramble," said Shiver.

"And Sprucie? Do you see him around?"

"We don't talk much about Sprucie; we never know who's listening. In his own mind, he's become *prominent*. He talks a lot, and some listen. By the way, what about Kas?"

"Kas is fine, but he didn't come back with us. We'll talk about that later, but listen, Shiver, we're supposed to be touring the Grove, so we'll have to go. If you meet Thorny, tell him I've been hoping to see him. Come on up to my form later and we'll talk, and I'm really sorry about Misty." Shiver

Journey *to* Hare Island

sat alone again on the shore, watching them go. Bramble and Dawn went south until they stood before a grove of tall spruce trees. "There's a meeting place in the centre of this stand," Bramble said. "Not much undergrowth, as you see, so no hares live there." They skirted the edge of the trees and emerged on the southern end of the meadow, close to the house. "Humans live there," said Bramble, pointing to the house, "but they don't bother us."

Dawn tried to identify the scents coming from the house, but they were strange to her. "What's a human?" she asked.

"It's hard to explain if you've never seen one. They're animals that stand on their hind legs. They can't run fast, but they have dogs. Dogs are something like coyotes. You'll see too soon."

At forms along the route, Bramble had called to individuals and occasionally was able to introduce Dawn to hares he knew. Usually, however, there was no answer, even though they saw hares sitting under the bushes. "Lots of empty forms and hares who don't want to talk," he said. "Not like the place I left. I've seen enough; let's go rest for a while."

In the early evening, Bramble and Dawn sat once more with the First Hare. "Well, what did you see?" he asked.

"Friends gone," said Bramble. "Empty forms. I've tried not to let myself think too much. It must have been a terrible winter?"

"What we feared came to pass," said the First Hare. He turned and said directly to Dawn, "I warned the community, and then I asked Bramble to go on a journey."

— 119 —

"Yes," said Bramble, "and I lost the elixir."

"I know you did, Bramble, but listen carefully; it's time to explain something and I don't want to be misunderstood: *The main purpose of the journey was to keep you from exposure to the disease.*" Bramble's head rose in confusion. The First Hare continued, "And why was this important? Because we had no way of knowing whether any young hares would survive here at the Grove. There had to be someone to ensure our future. I was afraid that if I told you, you would refuse to leave your friends. And another thing: Saving Dawn and not the elixir was the best decision of your journey. Dawn is important to you, of course, but she is also important to Alder Grove. Whether someone on Hare Island, thinking of our needs, had anything to do with you two getting together, I have no way of knowing, but I sense a helping hand. And I think, Bramble, the elixir had fulfilled its role when it brought you close to Alder Grove: There is more to life for hares than moon dust." The First Hare sat back, his expression indicating he had finished that topic. Then he said, "By the way, have you heard that there's a gathering tomorrow night?"

"No one mentioned it, First Hare. When did you call it?"

"I didn't. Someone else did. Does that surprise you?"

"Without your permission? Unheard of!"

"Welcome to Alder Grove. So many died this winter that old relationships broke down. We needed strong leadership. I was tired, and the two hares who might have replaced me died. Of course, someone is trying to fill the gap."

"From what Stormy told us, it's Sprucie," said Bramble.

"Exactly, and he seems to think the full moon tomorrow night will lend authority to his plans. I've been told he hopes to become First Hare. Failing that, he'll try to persuade some to follow him to a new location, and take power there. I don't have the energy to stop him. To rebuild, we do need young leadership, but I think you are the leader we need, Bramble, not Sprucie."

"Me? On my journey, Kas and then Dawn helped me; I'm not sure I could lead anyone on my own."

"Bramble, a true leader is never alone. I knew your friends saw you as a leader when I picked you to make the journey. I had asked around, 'Tell me the young hare you'd trust?' The answer I always got was 'Bramble.'"

For a brief moment, Bramble wished he and Dawn were living by themselves somewhere else, but he knew Alder Grove would always be home. He looked in resignation at Dawn and then at the First Hare. "And how did you imagine I could stop Sprucie?"

"Of course that's up to you, Bramble, but if I can get my old bones out to the spruce clearing tomorrow night, I'm going to recommend you as our new First Hare. That will at least start the crowd thinking. After that, I'm afraid it's up to you."

Bramble and Dawn went back to their forms, but Bramble kept jumping up and hopping around the small clearing. Trying to divert him, Dawn asked, "Do you really think someone on Hare Island plotted to get us together?"

"It would have to be Rowan," said Bramble.

"Or my father," said Dawn.

"Or both of them?" replied Bramble. "Rascals!"

"If you found out someone *had* arranged our getting together," asked Dawn, "would it change the way you feel about me?"

"Not in the least. No one forced us." Bramble started to laugh, and Dawn joined in.

But a short time later, Dawn saw Bramble's face cloud over again. "The elixir not as important after all?" he said. "And me a First Hare? With the turns my life has taken lately, nothing should surprise me, but I wasn't prepared for this. If I had to decide that First Hare thing tonight, I'd say *no*."

Chapter 25

A DIFFERENT JOURNEY

> *Every journey's end*
> *is the beginning of something else—*
> *Of another journey perhaps,*
> *In this or some other world.*
> —*Kas*

Early the next morning, while she and Bramble were stirring on their forms, Dawn said, "Bramble, I'll be happy with whatever decisions you make at the gathering."

Now they were eating near the lake, with a few more hares around than they had seen their first morning. Bramble heard someone approaching and looked up just as he was receiving a playful head butt, and a familiar voice said, "Move aside, you big ruffian, and introduce me to your friend." The two hares hopped around each other and ended up nose to nose.

"Dawn," said Bramble, "don't believe anything this hare tells you, but trust him with your life. This is Thorny, my littermate. We brought each other up." Dawn gave a polite dip of her head, as did Thorny.

"I don't mind admitting," Thorny said to Dawn, "that he did more of the bringing up. It's great to have him back in the

— 123 —

Grove." Dawn could see an obvious resemblance between the two, except that Bramble was a bit larger, and Thorny had no scar on his cheek. Thorny, who was facing the alders, suddenly tensed. He said in a low voice, "Sprucie must have seen you out here; he's coming with two cronies."

Sprucie had filled out some, but he still had a sharp face, and he was still small for an adult hare. His size, however, didn't stop him from speaking with confidence: "Well, Bramble, you're back from your jaunt, and I see you've found someone new along the way. Did you trade Kas for her?"

Bramble remembered how Sprucie had treated Kas, but he stayed calm. "This is Dawn, Sprucie. How have you been?"

"I've been fine, considering. We've had our problems, but some are learning to cope better than others." Sprucie drew a big breath and tried to stand tall. "We're trying to get organized, and I hope we can count on you and Thorny and, of course, Dawn, to support us."

"*Us?*" Bramble asked. "Does that include the First Hare?"

"You wouldn't know, Bramble, because you were away, but the First Hare did *not* lead well this winter." Sprucie swept one paw around the meadow. "You see how few hares are out here this morning? That should tell you something."

"Indeed it does, but the First Hare has been a good leader, and he didn't cause the sickness. You didn't tell me who the *us* includes."

"To be quite frank," Sprucie said, a note of irritation in his voice, "*many* in the Grove are asking *me* to lead."

"Sprucie, I confess I'm surprised."

"Surprised!" Sprucie dropped his veneer of politeness. "Where were you when we needed all the help we could get? So I can't look to you, or I suppose Thorny, for support?" He

Journey to Hare Island

looked over at Dawn and tried to smile. "I don't blame you, dear; you are most welcome to join us."

"Thanks for the offer," said Bramble. "In the meantime, if any one of your crowd accidentally looks at Dawn, he'll find himself swimming in a very cold lake."

The two hares with Sprucie moved toward Bramble, but Sprucie waved them off, and all three went quickly back into the alders. Bramble glared at them as they went. Dawn and Thorny looked at each other and smiled. "It's getting lighter," said Thorny. "We'd better get off the meadow, too. If you decide to say anything tonight, Bramble, you know you've got my support. Bye, Dawn." The smile was still visible in his eyes.

Bramble and Dawn spent the day talking to more of Bramble's acquaintances. They gathered that the First Hare still had a good deal of support, but it was hard to know whether that support would transfer to Bramble if his name came up at the gathering.

As they were going back to their forms for a few hours of rest, Bramble shook his head and looked at Dawn and said, "I wish I knew what I should do tonight."

When it was time for the gathering, Bramble and Dawn made their way south along the edge of the alders. Here and there clouds showed dark against the starlit heavens, but for now the moon shone brightly through the tops of the taller spruce trees. When they got to the clearing, the circle was forming. Sadly, it would be smaller than the one in the fall had been. Strawberry, who always led the chanting, had died in the winter, so there would be no chanting tonight. Bramble and

Dawn moved into the circle next to Thorny. Shiver joined them shortly after.

Sprucie stood inside the circle, trying to look as if he belonged there. When most of the Grove hares were present, he began to speak: "I take the liberty of doing the speaking because our First Hare is no longer able to function. Leadership is essential if we are to survive. You all know me; I suffered with you through this horrible winter. I was the one who pointed out how the First Hare had failed to protect us. Now I'm simply not able to turn down the requests from so many that I take a leadership role. Alder Grove may have seen its best years, but if you wish, I'm willing to stay here and lead. If you don't want to stay, I can take you to a place where there'll be more food and better protection from our enemies. In short, I'm willing to serve."

There were a few shouts of support for Sprucie, but then, to the great surprise of all present, Stormy was heard asking for passage through the circle, and the First Hare entered, slowly but with resolve, and took his accustomed place.

Bramble whispered to Dawn, "This is where I get to choose."

The First Hare looked around the circle, acknowledged some of the senior hares, and smiled at Bramble and Dawn. Then he looked up at the moon, now visible above the clearing. Finally he lifted his front paws, asking for quiet, and said, "Hares of Alder Grove, I surprised myself, and I'm sure you, by lasting through our tragic winter, but I'm now too old to carry on as First Hare. I thank you for the privilege of serving, but we must rebuild, and only a younger hare will have the energy needed." Sprucie rose in his place for a moment, and there were a few cheers. The First Hare ignored him and went on.

Journey *to* Hare Island

"Last fall, in the face of coming troubles, it was my responsibility to select a young hare with proven character and determination and send him on a difficult journey. I chose Bramble, who was accompanied by his friend Kas. I've had a chance to speak at length with Bramble since he returned. I'm amazed at the dangers he faced on our behalf, including crossing the lake as the ice was breaking up and fighting to the death with a hare intent on killing him and his new friend Dawn. So while we were struggling to live, Bramble, too, was facing grave dangers. And he survived. And he came home. What I can see from Bramble's experiences is that he has the courage and resourcefulness of a leader, one determined to do his duty for Alder Grove. I could say more, but I fear my strength is going, so I must return to my form. Before I go, however, I offer you my firm belief that you should choose Bramble as your First Hare."

As an excited chatter filled the clearing, the old hare rested his arm on Stormy's broad shoulders, and together they made their way out of the circle and down the path toward Alder Grove.

Sprucie jumped quickly to his feet. "I think we can ignore that interruption by someone whose time is past. And look who he recommends: a Swampie who left here when danger threatened and came home when the troubles were over. I remind you that I come from a family of leaders and that my grandfather was First Hare; I am not a Low Ender trying to climb above my place." He took a theatrical look over at Bramble.

There was a mixed reaction from the gathering, some cheers and some groans, but Bramble guessed that Sprucie had revealed more than he intended about his proposed leadership.

Bramble sighed, turned to Dawn, and asked, "How can I let someone who thinks that way become First Hare?" He rose and looked in turn at Thorny, at Shiver, and back at Dawn.

Finally, he moved into the centre of the circle. He was a big hare, but he seemed to grow even larger as he stood there and looked slowly around.

Meanwhile, a short way down the path to the Grove, the old First Hare and Stormy were sitting and listening. They heard Sprucie's comments and waited to hear what would happen. Several minutes passed. Then they heard Bramble's voice, loud and clear, and the old hare let out a long breath.

"It's true," said Bramble, "my early months were difficult. My littermate Thorny and I were often on the verge of starvation, or of being taken by one of our enemies. Fortunately, with the help of some of the older hares here tonight, we survived. I remember thinking that when I grew up, all I'd want would be enough food and the chance to lead an ordinary life here in the Grove, near the lake, with my friends. A part of me still yearns for that simple life, but I see now that things don't always work out the way we dream them to: the terrible sickness in Alder Grove, the dangerous journey I had to undertake, who could have known? And now the possible burden and challenge that our First Hare has suggested. I did not dream of becoming First Hare, and if I do, it will be your decision, not mine. Renewal will come to Alder Grove only in time, and with great effort. If I am chosen First Hare, we will begin tomorrow morning by cleaning our runs so that this spring our youngsters will have a better chance to survive. But they will survive, and Alder Grove will prosper. We owe this to our ancestors, and to the generations of snowshoe hares that must follow us. Let's not talk of leaving our home; let's talk only of renewal. Thank you for listening."

On the path leading back to the Grove, the old First Hare and his friend Stormy waited. After Bramble finished his statement, there was a period of silence. Then as they listened they heard hare voices, and the sound grew until it broke free of the spruce clearing, reached all the way back to Alder Grove, and then echoed out over the broad expanse of the lake: *Bramble, Bramble, BRAMBLE, BRAMBLE, BRAMBLE!*

Stormy said later that the old hare almost did a dance on the pathway. He looked up at the moon. Then he put his paw back on Stormy's shoulder and said, "It looks as though I can rest now. Let's go home."

Chapter 26
SPRING VISIT

Grampy, Evan, and Tessie sat on the front deck. "I can't believe this weather," said Evan, squinting up at the bright sky. "It's only April, and we can sit out here." The children and their parents were visiting Grampy for Easter, and the three on the deck were awaiting a call to dinner.

There were buds on the hardwoods but no leaves. Only the spruce and fir trees, and the grass on the edges of the meadow, were green; on their left, the bushes that stretched to the edge of the lake were still winter dark.

"See any hares yet this spring, Grampy?" asked Evan.

"I thought I saw some movement down there just now. We were seeing more a month or so ago, but not as many lately. They've had a hard couple of winters, but they'll come back. It's Easter, after all."

"You told us all that stuff with the story last fall, remember? That's why I was wondering how many there were," Evan said. Then he jumped from his chair and exclaimed, "Look! Down in the corner! Two snowshoe hares."

Tessie took up a pair of binoculars from the picnic table and said, "One has a mark on the side of his head, just like Bramble in the story. The other is smaller."

Journey *to* Hare Island

"Let's see the bins, Tessie," said Grampy. "Your eyes are better than mine." He watched for several minutes, then he shook his head. "Well, I'll be darned; they seem to come out to see you guys. I wondered if that one had survived the winter; he's been around for a few years. I'll bet there'll be young ones showing themselves in a couple of weeks."

A voice came from inside: "Only five minutes to wash up for dinner."

The old man glanced at the two children and saw both shoving something brown into their mouths. "What are you guys eating? If your parents catch you eating candy before dinner, you'll be in trouble."

"Just a chocolate Easter bunny," said Evan, "and I had only one Easter egg this morning."

"What?" roared Grampy, a smile on his face. "You're eating a bunny?"

Evan looked surprised, then guilty. "Didn't think about that."

They all laughed and got up to go in. Tessie took a last look down at the meadow. "Sorry, Bramble!" she yelled.

One hare sat up and looked toward the house, the mark on its cheek not so obvious in the spring sunshine, then he went back to eating.

Printed in Canada